NO BAIL FROM THE GRAVEYARD

Lew Pool was in the bail bonding business for his health as well as for the buck. Lew had picked up a bad case of the claustrophobia heebie-jeebies in the Korean War. And the only way he could get rid of his psycho-bug was to get his hands on a shady two-timer named Kreena.

Working near the jail, Lew figured that sooner or later he'd get a line on the whereabouts of the treacherous skunk who had the kind of talent for dirty work as kept the boys in blue busy.

And the day that a big purple car pulled up in front of his office and unloaded a bomb, Lew knew that Kreena was wise to him. The only question now was whether Lew could get his hands on that murderous devil before Kreena gave him a permanent mental cure — with a bullet.

TEDD THOMEY writes: "As a former police reporter for California dailies, I became quite interested in the unusual operations of bail bond offices. After interviewing a bondsman one night, it occurred to me that if such a man suffered from claustrophobia he would have a particularly trying time interviewing his clients behind bars . . .

"Like the bail bond business, the newspaper business can also be hazardous as I discovered one Christmas Eve in San Francisco. While interviewing a murder suspect in the back seat of a police car, I was nearly shot when a patrolman accidentally discharged the .32 caliber murder pistol. The bullet passed through the cushion near my elbow. Just like Lew Pool, I have carried a slight psychological scar ever since, growing extremely uncomfortable whenever anyone — police officer or private citizen — handles a firearm in my presence."

I WANT OUT

by

TEDD THOMEY

WILDSIDE PRESS

For J, with love.

CHAPTER I

You know how it is some mornings. That second cup of caffeine puts zip in your blood and skip in your step. So I kept my eye on the bull's-eye as I walked along Pacific Avenue. The bull's-eye in this case was one of the prettiest little posteriors I'd seen for months.

She wore a sky-blue skirt, made of a gleaming taffeta which hugged her lovingly, high-lighting the gentle to-and-fro motion as she stepped along on blue spike heels.

She was quite small, five feet or under, and she took such tiny steps I had to slow up to keep from walking into her.

At Pacific and Third Street, she paused uncertainly, then continued walking, and as she approached my place I knew it would be asking too much to expect her to stop there.

But she did.

She glanced up at my sign: *LEW POOL, Bail Bonds.*

She hesitated, and then I saw her glance at the signs of my competitors further up the street, and I knew the time had come for direct action.

I caught up with her.

"I'm Lew Pool," I said.

As she turned toward me, I was pleasantly surprised. She was oriental, her features small and perfect, her complexion a light cream color with just a hint of Filipino or Chinese in it. I could feel my adrenal glands start to vibrate cheerfully. I've taken a special interest in oriental women ever since the government gave me that all-expenses-paid junket to North Korea and the Yalu River.

"Got a problem?" I said, re-establishing what I hoped would look like poise on my foolish features.

"Yes," she said in excellent English. "Do you get people out?"

"I try," I said. "Shall we talk about it inside?"

I hated to look away from her, even for a moment, because I'd discovered that the sky-blue nylon sweater definitely was as attractive as I had expected. But I had to unlock the door, of course, and perform such other gentlemanly duties as dusting Billy's footprints off the chairs.

"It's my fiancé." She placed her beautiful bare legs closer together and smoothed her skirt with a quick, nervous gesture.

I refused to be disappointed. After all, there are many varieties of fiancés, ranging from A to A—Ardent to Asinine. And if I were lucky, hers might turn out to be one of the latter.

"He's in jail?" I asked.

She nodded.

"I'll need some information." I picked up a sheet of office paper and a ball-point pen. "I'll need his name, age, address, and the charges."

"Certainly." She nodded and said something else which I missed; because just then I decided her eyes were entirely too large and too Dresden blue to be real. And they were in stunning contrast to her high oriental cheekbones and the glossy darkness of her long black hair which she wore in a cute pony tail.

"Would you repeat that, please?" I asked.

She frowned delightfully. "Yes, of course. His name is Felix Pia. He's thirty-six," she said. "He lives at 2828 East Thirteenth Street. And I believe they arrested him because he was in a fight last night."

"What kind of a fight?" I said. "A brawl, a riot or just a plain donnybrook? If it's simple assault, we won't have any trouble."

She didn't reply at once, but rose from the chair, walked to the office front door and closed it.

"I don't know what kind of a fight," she said.

I got up from my desk, walked to the door and opened it. Then I returned to the desk.

"You weren't there?" I said.

"No," she said as she stood and walked to the door. "I didn't even know about it until Felix's sister phoned this morning, all excited."

She closed the door again and gracefully returned to her chair.

When I rose again, she held up a slim hand.

"Please leave it closed," she asked.

Well, it was a balmy California morning, with April only a couple of days away, and since she had on that sky-blue nylon sweater she couldn't be too chilly, so I walked over again and opened the door. And I didn't feel like explaining to her why I *had* to have the door open.

"I'm sort of an idiot," I said, giving her the old fib. "I like to gulp fresh air the way a fish gulps H$_2$O."

"Oh?" she said. "Is that why you look sort of like a hammerhead shark?"

From the cool way she said it I couldn't tell whether she was kidding, or whether by some obscure feminine talent she had seen through my lie. I am ugly, of course, in a fascinating way; but I'm no hammerhead shark, not even at eight o'clock on Monday morning.

"Your round," I said, grinning my best grin, which didn't effect her in the slightest.

She went to the door and closed it again and suddenly I realized she was extremely nervous and had been trying all along to conceal it. I decided it was time for me to act less like Lew Pool, the working girl's Casanova, and more like Lew Pool, the workingman's bail bondsman.

"I'll need your name also," I said in a brisk, business-like tone.

"It's Ti-lo," she said. "With a hyphen."

"Got it," I said. "First name or last?"

"First," she said. "My last name is Sullivan. My mother was Filipino," she explained, "and my daddy was Irish."

I asked semi-harmless questions like her address and phone number.

She refused to tell me until I insisted for the third time that the information was strictly for my business records.

Then the door got to bothering me again and I walked over and opened it.

That really put the freeze on.

"Must this take so long?" she demanded, giving me an irritated look. "And how much is this going to cost me?"

"It all depends," I said. "If your boy friend has been a model inmate we'll have him out in a few hours. If he's been playful, if he bit the jailer's hand or spit in his ear, it'll take longer."

I dialed the cop-shop number and talked to Winebrenner, the booking sergeant. After he flipped through a few arrest reports, he informed that one Felix Oretga Pia was being held on a 4130.

"Thanks," I said, hanging up.

"Not bad," I told her. "We'll have him out this afternoon."

She wasn't looking at me. She was gazing at the open door and as she rose from her chair again I assumed she was going to continue our little I'll-close-it-you-open-it game.

And then the explosion came.

There was a tremendous flash just outside the open door and a tremendous noise which thundered back and forth between the walls of the small office, knocking down my framed bondsman's certificate, blowing a stack of receipts off the bookcase and making my eardrums vibrate like organ pipes.

Ti-lo screamed once. She reached out for the chair to support herself, missed by a yard and toppled.

She landed smack on her little taffeta-covered posterior, rolled over once and lay still.

I sprang around the desk, stepped over her and looked out through the clouds of blue smoke which were billowing around the doorway. I saw a heliotrope-colored car, it looked like a new Buick. It was going like hell, and was much too far away for me to read the license number.

I knelt down beside Ti-lo, but I couldn't see a mark on her.

CHAPTER II

SHE WAS COVERED with tiny, ragged bits of paper. More of the little fragments were floating through the office, settling on me and the furnishings. I sniffed at the antiseptic sulphurous odor hanging in the air. It was familiar. I picked up some of the bits of paper. Then I strode outside and examined a black, flash-burned area on the moss-green stucco wall near the doorway and my suspicions were confirmed.

A giant firecracker had caused the uproar, not a bomb.

I picked Ti-lo up and it was a pleasure. It was indeed a pleasure to slide one arm beneath her bare, warm knees and the other across her dainty shoulder blades. She weighed about as much as a piece of Melba toast. As I carried her to the divan, her face was quite near to mine. And if it does nothing else, a close-up like that will prove a lady's age once and for all. I decided Ti-lo couldn't be a day over twenty. She wore no make-up except claret-colored lipstick. She would never need make-up, simply because her skin was as fine-textured as a baby's.

I placed her on the divan, propping her feet up on the armrest to get the blood flowing back to her head. I removed her spike-heeled shoes and began to gently massage her feet. Then I brushed the bits of firecracker paper from her hair and off her skirt. I would like to say that my gentlemanly instincts prevented me from brushing off the lovely front of her sky-blue nylon sweater but this would not be exactly true. I was prevented from doing so by the fact that she was beginning to wake up.

She didn't say anything foolish like "What happened?" or "Where am I?"

The first thing she noticed were her bare feet. She took a swing at me and began shrieking at the top of her lungs. "Where are my shoes! My beautiful blue shoes!"

She jumped off the divan and began shagging me around the office, pummeling my back.

And at that moment in came half a dozen uniformed gentlemen from the cop shop across the street. I don't blame them for standing there gawking at what certainly was a ridiculous scene. Without her spike heels, Ti-lo was a pint-sized four-feet-eleven and I'm a gallon-sized five-feet-eleven with a chest like a butane tank.

She finally spied the cops, pointed a claret fingernail at me and yelped: "Arrest this man! He stole my shoes!"

One of the John Laws advanced toward me with a grim I'm-bucking-for-sergeant expression on his face.

"Relax," I said.

I found her shoes at the side of the divan and handed them to her.

I turned back to the Johns. "She fainted when the firecracker went off. All I did was massage her tootsies to bring her out of it."

Ti-lo abruptly said: "Oh!"

She plopped down on the divan, her face pale, her shoulders shaking, and I could see that she was remembering the shock of the explosion and how she had keeled over like a broken sunflower.

It took her a minute to get her breath and composure

back. Then she slipped on her blue shoes and smiled up at the half-circle of Johns.

"I'm very sorry," she said. "I guess I—"

"Sure, one of the boys said. "It was quite a bang and we ain't blaming you for losing your temper."

He turned to me and his tone became gruff again. "Any idea who done it? Some pal of yours, maybe, joking around?"

I shook my head. "No pal of mine. I think it was tossed from a heliotrope Buick."

"A heliotrope Buick?" He wrote it down in his notebook, and then led his gang outside. They milled around on the sidewalk for another minute, studied the flash-burn on the wall and then they trotted two-by-two back to the cop shop.

I sat down behind the desk. "Well, Miss Sullivan," I said, "shall we go on? Or would you rather try one of my competitors down the street?"

"No, thanks, Mr. Pool." She produced the friendliest smile she'd given me all morning. "I'm sorry about the way I acted. And I'm grateful for the way you picked me up from the floor."

"Don't be so formal," I said. "Call me Lew. And any time you want to faint, you go right ahead. I'll be there to pick you up."

"I'm sure you've had lots of practice." She said it a little more sweetly than necessary.

I let it pass and I saw that I would have to keep alert around her because she was plenty sharp.

"What about that Buick?" I said. "You know anybody who owns a lavender one?"

"No."

"You sure you didn't expect something to happen?"

"No."

"Why did you keep closing the door?"

"It was drafty."

They were all logical answers. I knew if I were to press

the point further and ask her why she was now willing to let the door remain open, she would undoubtedly have a ready answer for that one, too.

I dialed Winebrenner, the booking sergeant, and asked him if he's seen Billy.

"He's standing right here," Winebrenner said. "He's checking out in a few minutes."

"Put him on, will you?"

There was a brief delay and then I heard Billy's cheerful, beer-soaked baritone.

"Top o' the mawrnin' to ye, Lew."

"You're late," I said, "and you're keeping a client waiting."

"I'm on me way, Lew. We had a mite o' excitement here this mawrnin'. I'll be tellin' ye all about it."

He hung up with a happy crash of the receiver and in a minute I saw him through the doorway as he limped toward the office from across the street. When he came in he wore his big grin; he also wore his surplus navy pea jacket and his big woolly tweed cap.

He nodded at me, removed the monstrous cap and bowed with stiff-backed elegance in Ti-lo's direction.

"Mawrnin', ma'am," he said. "I trust the boy here has been takin' care o' ye properly durin' me absence?"

Well, that's Billy McCorkell for you. You'd think he owned the business instead of being my assistant. He's the kind of guy who usually gets crocked on Fridays and I rarely see him again until Monday. First I bail him out of the drunk tank and then he helps me bail out a few others. It's a very silly arrangement, but it works remarkably well since Billy touts the other drunks onto buying their bonds from me.

"Here now, ma'am," he said sympathetically. "What's that no good Lew been doin' to ye?"

And without another word he walked over and began dusting the bits of firecracker paper off her sky blue nylon sweater. He was very careful to brush only at her shoulders. Also, he was careful not to breathe on her because one sniff of his breath would have dropped her like a pole-axed steer.

I let him have his fun and when he finished I introduced them.

"Her fiancé's in the lock-up," I added, "and I want you to get him out."

I handed him the necessary papers which I'd filled in and twenty-five dollars, which I removed from my billfold.

"The gentleman's name is Felix Ortega Pia," I said. "He's in on a 4130."

"I'm on me way," Billy said.

He tugged his woolly cap down around his ears, limped toward the doorway and then halted.

"Speakin' o' the lock-up," he said, "I didn't get around to tellin' you o' the excitement. Some fella got himself shot this mawrnin'. And him behind bars, he was."

"Well, fancy that," I said, keeping my face straight. "I trust you found plenty of loose beer-money in his pants?"

"Shame on ye," Billy scowled. "I wasn't even in the same cell with the poor helpless fella. And ye shouldn't say such things in front of the little lady there. She'll be thinkin' I'm a drinkin' man."

Ti-lo's eyes twinkled with sudden mischief.

"Sure an' ye know I'd niver be thinkin' that." Her brogue was twice as thick as his.

Billy whisked his cap off, tossed it gleefully and caught it behind his back. Then he jigged his way across the office, bent near her and cupped a hand around his ear.

"Would ye be repeatin' that, miss?"

"Faith and St. Patrick's shillelagh!" she said. "I kin tell by yer foine fair face that ye ain't had a drop o' the Irish since Paddy fell in the well."

Billy whooped and hit me on the jaw with his cap. "Did

ye hear 'em, Lew? Did ye hear them angel's words?"

They volleyed foine's, niver's and ye's back and forth like tennis balls for several enthusiastic minutes and then Billy remembered his mission and apologized for keeping her waiting. He departed with joy spread all over his red cheeks. Ti-lo and I sat without speaking for a moment and watched him as he crossed the street, trying manfully with each step to minimize his limp.

"I think I've changed my opinion of you," she said.

"Now what have I done?" I said, wincing a little.

"You can't be as bad as I thought," she said. "Not if you let a wonderful old man like that work for you."

I wasn't just surprised. I was pleased, but I tried not to let it show.

"He's not so old," I said. "He's only in his sixties."

"Does his leg hurt him?" she asked.

"Not any more. The VA took it off below the knee a few years back."

She drew in her breath softly.

"He's better off," I said. "He carried fragments in it for years."

"From the war?"

I nodded. "World War I. They gassed him, too, but he never complains. He's pretty proud of his cough. You ought to hear him sometime. After he's had six or seven beers, he coughs up a storm. Sounds like a dragon with a Model-T caught in its throat."

We laughed together, sharing a good moment.

We made small talk until we saw Billy coming around the corner of the cop shop across the street.

When he entered the office, his face was serious and his voice subdued.

"Let me talk to ye outside, will ye, Lew?"

We excused ourselves and went out on the sidewalk.

"It's pretty terrible," Billy whispered. "It's him that got shot, that Felix fella."

"Her boy friend?" I whispered. "Are you sure?"

"Sure an' I'm sure!" He looked sadly toward the doorway. "It's ye who'll have to tell th' poor thing, Lew. Her little Felix fella is as dead as th' poor clay itself."

Billy crossed himself and hung his head.

Unfortunately he never quite learned the art of whispering. His rough voice carried inside the office and I knew, by the crashing sound, that she had heard.

When we dashed inside, she was lying flat on the floor again.

CHAPTER III

ALL WE HAD to revive her with was a can of warm beer. I propped her head against the divan's armrest and forced a little into her mouth. She swallowed pretty well for a moment, then she gasped and came up fighting, blinking her eyes rapidly.

I stepped back so she couldn't swing at me and pointed at her feet.

"They're okay," I said. "Look."

She looked at her blue shoes, but this time they weren't important. She covered her face, weeping into her hands so quietly she could scarcely be heard.

"I'm sorry," I said. "I'm very sorry you had to hear it that way."

" 'Tis I should apologize," Billy added. "I kin no more whisper than a cat kin fly."

I gave her my handkerchief and she dried her eyes.

"I'm all right," she said, swallowing.

None of us spoke for a minute or so. She dug into her tiny purse to find her lipstick. I watched her carefully, unable to decide how strongly she was being affected by the news.

"Care to talk about it a little?" I asked her.

"I suppose so," she said.

"Was Felix a Filipino?"

She nodded.

I made a large mental note. As far as I was concerned that was the No. 1 fact so far in the whole business. I decided to forego subtlety for a moment and see how much more I could find out.

"Did you love him?" I asked.

"Fer cryin' out loud," Billy scolded, "can't ye keep yer elephant feet off the poor girl's feelin's?"

"It's all right, Billy," she said.

"Did you love him?" I repeated.

"I don't know. I—I'm mixed up."

"How long did you know him?"

"About a year."

"When did you become engaged?"

That one bothered her. Her blue eyes glanced down at her shoes and then out the open door.

"Two days ago. On my birthday."

I looked at the third finger of her left hand. "Didn't he give you a ring?"

That one bothered her too. "He was as short of money. He said I'd get the ring later this week."

"And what did he give you for your birthday?"

Instead of replying, she plucked a balled-up Kleenex from her purse and dabbed at her eyes.

I decided I needed to know a lot more about an alleged fiancé who wouldn't award a delectable doll like Ti-lo either a ring or a birthday present.

I gave her what I hoped was a gentle look. "Can you handle a few more questions or do you want me to shut up?"

"She wants ye to shut up," Billy said.

"Kindly keep your nose out of this," I told him.

"It's all right, Billy," she said. "Mr. Pool's trying to help."

"Call me Lew," I said.

She didn't change her expression. "You wanted to ask me something else?"

"Yes. Do you have any idea why anyone would want to kill Felix? And why they would risk doing it in jail?"

She shook her head.

"Do you think there's any connection between his death and the firecracker?"

She shook her head again and her glossy black pony tail danced.

"One last question," I said. "Did you ever hear of a Filipino called Kreena?"

I waited anxiously for her answer to that one, far more anxiously than she could ever guess.

"Who?" she said.

I spelled it out for her. "K-r-e-e-n-a."

Once more the pony tail shimmered as she shook her head. "No," she said. "Do you think he killed Felix?"

"I doubt it," I said. "I just thought I'd ask."

We sat for another minute without speaking, occupied with our individual thoughts. Billy took the can of warm beer off my desk, drank half of it and made a face.

"Delicious," he said. "But niverth'liss, Mr. Pool, I'd like to know when ye'll be a puttin' in the refrigerator."

"Niver," I replied.

"Warm beer's bad fer me," he complained. He coughed pitifully into his woolly cap, but for him it wasn't much of a cough, sounding no worse than a leaky inner tube being blown up by a leaky tire pump.

Ti-lo rose from the divan and walked to the doorway. For a thoughtful moment, she looked across the street at the cop shop.

She came back to the desk and looked directly into my eyes.

"What are you going to do about it?" she asked.

"About what?"

"About Felix?"

"What can *I* do?"

"You're a detective, aren't you?"

It was my turn to do a little head shaking. "I'm not a detective and I have no desire to be one. I'm a bail bondsman and it's a nice, safe business and I want to keep it that way."

"You mean you won't even *try* to find out what happened?"

"I didn't say that."

"Then you *will* find out what happened to Felix?"

"I'll try."

"Will you want some money? I have a little."

I shook my head again. "Let's not let commercialism intrude into what could be a beautiful friendship. Besides, I don't mail my bills out till the last week of the month."

"Billy, how about getting the details on what happened to Felix?"

Ti-lo pouted prettily. "You won't go yourself?"

"I'd rather stay here with you," I said. "You look like you still need comforting."

"Watch him, miss, when he starts that comfortin' routine," Billy warned as he walked out the doorway. Suddenly he turned and beckoned to me.

I followed him and this time we stood far enough away from the door so she couldn't overhear.

"Ye know I'll be no good over there," Billy said. "I'm okay at gettin' th' drunks out but I don't know nuthin' about dead men and I'm not wantin' to know."

I scowled at him. "You know damn well I can't go."

"Sure and maybe ye better," he said. "Sure and how d'ye think ye'll ever be gettin' cured if ye don't meet it head on?"

"I don't think so," I said.

He tapped me vigorously on the chest. "And what about Kreena? Ain't this the first good opportunity ye've had? With two Chinamen in the case already, ye might well run into a few more."

"Filipinos," I corrected. "And I suppose you're right."

"Tis as clear as Mrs. McCarthy's wash water." He shoved me in the general direction of the cop shop. "Don't worry about it—don't even think about it—and ye'll be all right."

I went, but I was none too happy about it. I was all right so long as I was in the cop shop's main lobby, because the side doors to the street were open. The jail, unfortunately, is on the seventh floor and as soon as I got in the elevator I had that hemmed-in feeling. It was as if the walls of the elevator were closing in on me, starting to crush me. I tried very hard to ignore those damn walls even though I knew it would no no good. Claustrophobia can't be ignored. By the time we got to the seventh floor, I felt like I was in a coffin, a narrow metal coffin jammed so close around my body and head that I could bite into the the cheap, forty-cents-a-yard satin the undertaker had lined it with.

I felt better, but not much better, as I stepped into the jail's main hallway. The sight of all those gray-painted bars and walls made me feel nauseated. There wasn't an open door anywhere. The elevator was the only way in and out, and it had departed after depositing me in the hall.

I walked over to the booking desk.

"Pia was my client," I told Sergeant Winebrenner. "Where's the action? I'm in a hurry."

I always talk fast when I feel lousy and Winebrenner frowned at me.

"Okay, okay," he said in a fatherly tone. "Calm down, Lew. Calm down."

He led the way to the drunk tank, passing through two

sets of heavy iron gates which he unlocked and then re-locked as we walked along. The locks snapping behind me, made me remember the filthy black hole where I had spent fourteen months in solitary.

I figured I could take maybe ten minutes of this—no more.

There was a gang of guys in the drunk tank. Most of them were Johns, uniformed cops and plainclothes detectives. They were busy taking pictures, measuring distances and gabbing among themselves.

"Where is he?" I asked Winebrenner. "Where's Felix?"

"Across the street at Clapper's," Winebrenner said. "In the icebox."

"What about his stuff? His clothes and personal stuff?"

"Lowney took 'em. He's down in Detectives."

I stood there a few minutes, feeling sick. The Johns had used yellow chalk to draw the figure of a man on the concrete floor. It was unintentionally a Virgil Partch-type of thing—the head too large, the legs and arms stubby and thick. From the way it was bent in the middle I assumed Felix had been sitting on the floor, his back against the inside bars. There was another chalk line drawn on the floor to represent the path of the bullet. It originated in a large cell along the far south wall, passed through still another cell and then entered the drunk tank.

"It hit him in the back?" I asked Winebrenner.

"Yeah."

"Did he say anything before he died?"

"Not a thing."

"Who was in the other cell, the one where the gun was fired?"

"Four guys," Winebrenner said. "They got 'em down in Detectives."

"You find the gun?"

Winebrenner shook his head.

"Don't you consider that a little embarrassing?"

"Why should we?"

"Where's your professional pride?" I said. "Isn't it kind of sloppy of you guys to let some citizen sneak a gun in here, knock off another citizen and then hide the gun—right under your big noses?"

He merely blinked at me, but I could tell I'd gotten to him, because above his dark blue collar his plump neck was turning red.

I grinned at him, turned to watch one of the Johns flash another picture and then abruptly I felt sicker and the gray bars started closing in on me, like a platoon of thin soldiers marching toward me from four directions.

I leaned against Winebrenner's heavy shoulder.

"I'm sick," I said. "Let's get out of here."

"You and your big yap," he said. "I oughta let you stay here till you molt, like a pigeon with the pip."

He didn't mean it. He started walking fast, leading me through the mob of Johns and out the two gates. He's a good guy, the best friend I've got in the Police Department. He knows my trouble and what to do about it.

He got me to the elevator, punched the wall button and kicked the door hard in case the operator was parked somewhere between floors reading a girlie magazine. It was a long minute, with the bars squeezing in on me. I was afraid I was going to disgrace myself and throw up on Winebrenner's clean, gray-painted floor.

When the elevator arrived, he rode down with me, telling the operator not to stop at other floors. The operator did not take kindly to this, complaining all the way down; his panel was lit up like a whisky display.

Winebrenner led me out the side door and I slumped down on the steps, praising the lord for the great outdoors, with its wholesome carbon monoxide and fresh smog.

CHAPTER IV

I REFUSED the cigarette Winebrenner offered, then I changed my mind and lit one. It tasted rotten, like I expected, and I threw it away. I sat there for about five minutes and then I stood up. I felt wobbly, but I wanted to get the job done.

"Where do you think you're going?" Winebrenner asked as I hobbled down the steps.

"Didn't you say Felix is at Clapper's?"

"Yeah." He made a pitying clucking sound with his tongue. "You're in no shape to go over there. You'll get the heebie jeebies again."

"I'll only stay a minute," I said.

"Why in the blazes are you so interested? What's in it for you?"

"Filipinos," I replied.

"Hmmmm," he said. "Kreena?"

"Maybe."

He shook his head. "It's an awful long shot."

"I've got patience."

"You'll need it," he said.

He knew I might also need more propping up, so he volunteered to accompany me on the block-long walk along Third Street to Clapper's, the mortuary which got a good share of the cop-shop business.

Arriving at Clapper's, we went in through a side door and down to the basement. At the preparation room entrance, I wedged one of the two swinging doors open with a triangle of wood the attendants use when rolling corpses in and out on wheeled stretchers. I felt all right while we were in the main room, with that open door behind me. When we passed into the icebox section, with its heavy closed door, I could feel things cramping me again.

An attendant led us to the table where they were tieing an identification tag on Felix's big toe. He lay there on his back. He was a small, brownish man in his mid-thirties. I saw that the Virgil Partch-like sketch the Johns had made on the jail floor was pretty accurate. Felix had a too-large head on a too-small body and his legs and arms were short and stubby.

I wondered again why a doll like Ti-lo would become engaged to such a man.

"Show him the hole," Winebrenner said to one of the attendants.

They tilted Felix to one side and I was able to see the small dot on his back, directly behind his heart. They had washed the blood off and all that remained was the neat bullet hole, its edges a charred black.

"The slug's still in him?" I asked.

"Small caliber," the attendant said. "We'll find it okay."

The walls started undulating and closing toward me once more, but it wasn't as bad as in the jail, because here I could walk out when I chose.

"Okay," I told Winebrenner. "I've seen it."

We returned to the cop shop. I thanked him for his help and assured him that I was all right. He went back to his desk.

I stayed outside for awhile. When my nerves had calmed sufficiently, I went up the steps to Detectives on the second floor. I asked the desk man to tell Inspector Lowney I wanted to see him.

I had to wait over thirty minutes. The detectives make up the elite of the cop-shop caste system. These boys love their position, savoring their "ascendancy" over the lower forms of life. It's probably not necessary for me to mention that they place bail bondsmen lowest on their list, a step below such assorted creeps as private investigators, newspapermen and stoolies.

The waiting room was okay, it opened directly onto a staircase. When I entered Inspector Lowney's den, however, matters were much too cozy. The office was about eight-by-eight and fogged over with thick, blue cigarette smoke.

I left the door open behind me, but Inspector Lowney promptly slammed it shut. He then sat behind his desk and gazed at me as if I were something which had floated up from the sewer. He wore a well-tailored, black Dacron suit and his dark hair was parted with infuriating accuracy. His face was all points—pointed chin, nose and ears! A cigarette was held tightly between his lips and he toyed with an unlighted one, rolling it around between his fingers.

"Make it quick," he snapped. "We're interrogating."

"Pia was a client of mine," I said. "I'd like to see his personal effects."

"Oh, you would, would you?" Lowney sucked so hard on the cigarette the ash grew a half-inch.

"I'd also like a look at the four guys who were in the cell where the gun was fired."

"Oh, you would, would you?" He geysered blue smoke at me. "And what will you trade for such a look?"

"Information," I said.

He shrugged. "I'm listening."

"His fiancée's in my office," I said. "Her name's Ti-lo Sullivan. While we were talking, some jokers in a heliotrope-colored Buick roared by and tossed a firecracker practically in the door."

"So?" he said.

"It happened just about the time Felix Pia was shot. I don't think it was a coincidence."

Lowney tilted his head and his eyes narrowed thoughtfully. While he made a few notes on a pad, I eased the door open about a foot and immediately the office's walls went back into their true perspective.

"It isn't much," Lowney said, "but we'll look into it.

There can't be too many heliotrope-colored Buicks in town."

He took a key from his pocket and unlocked the door at the opposite side of his office.

"Take a peek," he said. "Keep it short."

He stood beside me while I glanced into the interrogation room. There were six men present—two detectives and the four suspects from the jail cell. I quickly brushed my eyes over three of the suspects. They were run-of-the-jail toughs, with boozy faces, long sideburns and they needed shaves. The fourth man was far more interesting.

He was a Filipino.

He was about thirty-one or thirty-two, with long sleek hair and brown eyes shiny as hard candy. His nose was exceedingly flat, possibly a gift of Mother Nature but more probably the result of constant hammering in a boxing ring. He wore a white shirt, open at the throat, and his yellow necktie was stuffed into the breast pocket of his avocado green suit.

"That's enough for now," Lowney said, closing and locking the door.

"What's his name?" I said. "The Filipino."

Lowney looked at his note pad. "Harold Pablo. Still uses the name King Harold, the name he fought under as a featherweight. Now works as a cook."

"Is he your prime suspect?"

Lowney stubbed out his cigarette, lit the one he'd been toying with and got out a third one which he rolled around in his fingers.

"Maybe," he said, "I haven't got time to talk. So if you'll kindly—"

He glanced at the door.

I didn't take the hint.

"What are the charges?" I said. "What are you holding those four on?"

"An open charge," he snapped. "If the tests prove out,

it'll be suspicion of murder. Now beat it and let me get some work done."

"Not yet," I said. "You've forgotten the other half of our deal. I want to see Pia's personal effects."

"We had no deal. Beat it."

"Don't get nasty," I said, "or I'll drop over to the squad room and tell the boys how Inspector Lowney tried to ravish a redhead at the 222 Club."

His face turned the color of a tomato can label. He was too drunk that night to remember what happened, but actually his conduct had been quite innocent. He had stumbled while rising from his table and his hand struck the back of the scantily-clad girl seated at the next table. She was one of the club strippers and it certainly wasn't his fault that she had a trick fastener at the back of her strapless bra. The bra popped off like a flapping dove, revealing her in all her rosy-tipped glory. And Inspector Lowney had promptly passed out.

"Damn you," he said.

He stormed out of the office, slammed the door and locked it.

He didn't have to do it, but it was his way of getting back at me.

A minute passed. Another.

Then another minute passed. I jumped up and tried both doors. Both were locked. I couldn't breathe and I couldn't think.

I stumbled to the window and tried to open it, but it was stuck.

I picked up the chair, swung it twice and smashed out the upper and lower panes.

I sat down on the chair in front of the window and let the breeze blow on me.

Both doors flew open simultaneously.

Inspector Lowney dashed in through one and the two

detectives piled in through the other from the interrogation room.

They stared at the snaggle-toothed fragments of glass remaining in the window and they also stared at me.

"You idiot!" Lowney roared. "What'd you do that for?"

I tilted the chair back. I almost felt fine.

"You ought to know better than lock me up," I grinned. "I go stir crazy."

"Why you—!" Lowney was so mad he couldn't talk. "I'll—"

"Ah, ah, ah!" I reminded him cheerfully. "Or should I say bra, bra, bra?"

He remembered. He spun on his heel and glowered at the other two Johns.

"Don't stand there like a couple of apes," he said. "Beat it!"

They performed orderly about-faces and marched back into the interrogation room.

Lowney flung a large Manila envelope on the desk.

"Here's his stuff," he said. "Look at it and then leave me in peace!"

Opening the envelope, I dumped Felix Pia's effects out onto the desk. It was the usual miscellany of a man's pockets —sixty-five cents in change, a ring of keys, a pencil stub, a newspaper recipe for Lobster Cantonese, a tan leather bill-fold, a handkerchief, a business card, a comb with several long oily hairs caught in the plastic teeth, and a second newspaper clipping telling the arrival date of the S. S. Caledonia from Quezon City.

"Okay," Lowney said. "You've seen it all."

He started putting the objects back in the envelope.

"Hold it," I said. "I'm not through."

I pushed his hand aside and picked up the business card, noticing as I did so that it had fallen atop a green-corroded key which was not connected to the main ring. I glanced at the card face and saw the words: *CHARLES HORONDO,*

Business Opportunities Broker. Flipping the card over, I saw
the letter "S" in feminine script on the back and below it
a phone number.

I performed two manipulations. One was mental: I memorized the phone number.

The second was physical. I stuck the card under Lowney's
pointed nose and asked: "Ever hear of this guy?"

And at the same time my other hand palmed the key
off the desk.

"Never heard of him," Lowney said.

He snatched the card from my fingers and shoved it and
the rest of the objects into the envelope. Then he seized
my shoulder and propelled me through the door.

"And stay out!" he said.

I didn't mind the bum's rush. Somehow I felt I had the
most important thing—the key.

CHAPTER V

As I WALKED back across the street to my cottage-sized
office, I examined the key closely. It was a medium-size door
key, made of a darker than average brass. Across the rounded
end were oriental characters and the design of a kite. It
was a fish-shaped kite and its string coiled gracefully all
around the face of the key. From the amount of green
corrosion in the design crevices, I judged the key to be quite
old and undoubtedly made by hand somewhere in Asia.

I placed it in one of the leather compartments in my bill-
fold. As I approached the office door, which was closed, I
was greeted by the wail of Billy's harmonica.

I opened the door and was fairly impressed by the scene
within. There were five empty beer cans in an orderly row on
my desk. Billy was sitting on the divan; he was playing his
harmonica. Ti-lo was trying to jig to the tune in the small

space between the desk and the divan. Billy stopped between notes to cough and wheeze and Ti-lo stopped between steps to sip from the can of beer she was holding.

She spied me standing in the doorway and saluted me with the can.

"Good morning again," she said. "And what did you find out?"

I took the can from her and drained the little that was left.

"Beer isn't good for little colleens," I said. "Not at 11 a.m."

"Spoil sport," she pouted.

I walked over to Billy and slipped the harmonica out of his mouth.

"What's the matter with you?" I scowled. "At least you could've waited till this afternoon."

" 'Tis a wake we're havin'," he said. " 'Tis a wake fer poor Felix."

" 'Tis a lousy beer bust," I said, "and you should be ashamed of yourself. They'll lock you up for contributing to the delinquency of a minor."

"I've been twenty-one for two days," Ti-lo said.

"Go get us six more cans," Billy said. "An' gimmee back me accordion."

"You miserable idiot," I told him. "I'll bet you wheedled the beer money from her."

He didn't reply. He pulled his cap all the way down over his eyes, sighed a beery sigh and went to sleep.

I knocked the cans from the desk into the wastebasket and wrote down the phone number I had memorized from the card that had been among Felix's personal effects.

"You're mean," Ti-lo said. "You're mean to that poor old man. And besides, you're a party-pooper."

"Shut up," I told her pleasantly, "I have to make a phone call." I paused. "And besides, I think you'd make a better appearance if you showed a little remorse over what happened to Felix."

"You're mean to me, too!" she wailed.

She sat down on the divan beside Billy, leaned her head back and closed her eyes.

I dialed the number. After half a dozen rings, an operator answered and informed me that the number was disconnected.

I was neither disappointed or surprised. I called the phone company and asked to speak to Miss Viking, one of the supervisors.

"May I help you?" Miss Viking asked after a moment.

"You sure can, honey," I said. "This is Lew Pool, remember me?"

"Of course."

"I've been trying to call a number, HArrison 1-5843, but they tell me it's disconnected. Would you do me a favor, honey, and tell me what the address for that number is?"

"It's against the rules, Mr. Pool."

"I know, honey, but couldn't you do me a favor, for old time's sake?"

I noticed that Ti-lo, still leaning back against the divan headrest, was watching me through her eyelids which were open about one-thousandth of an inch. Each time I said the word "honey" her eyes opened a little bit further. There was no way for her to know of course, that Miss Viking was approximately fifty-eight years old with a face like a beaver's, including the whiskers.

"I suppose I do owe you a favor," Miss Viking said. "After all, you did get Walter out."

Her brother Walter, an obstinate cuss, had been locked up one night for refusing to sign a citation for jaywalking.

"It will take a few minutes," Miss Viking added. "Will you wait?"

"I could wait all day for you, honey," I said.

Ti-lo's Irish blue eyes were now completely open and they gazed at me coldly during the entire interval while I waited for Miss Viking to return to the phone.

"Here it is," Miss Viking said. "It's 9 El Portal. And don't you dare ever tell anybody where you got it."

I wrote the address down. "I won't, honey."

"You naughty boy," Miss Viking giggled. "Why do you keep calling me that?"

"Because you're so sweet," I said. "Goodbye, honey."

I hung up and looked at Ti-lo. "Does the address 9 El Portal mean anything to you? Did Felix ever mention it to you?"

She shook her head and the glossy dark ponytail glistened in the sunlight streaming in the open door.

"It doesn't mean a thing, *honey*," she said icily.

I dug the oriental key from my pocket and handed it across the desk to her.

"Did you ever see that before? It was among Felix's things."

She turned it over in her fingers, examining it.

"I've never seen it before, *honey*," she said.

"Why act so peeved?" I said. "What'd I do?"

"I don't like you," she said. "I don't like the way you sweet-talk girls."

"Maybe I have reasons," I said. "I'm still trying to find out about you and Felix."

She gazed down at the key in her palm. "I've been thinking about that. I guess I didn't really love Felix."

"Then why did you become engaged?"

"Because—" she hesitated, "because I felt sorry for him."

"Would you have married him?"

"No. He felt so bad that night at the Plum that I wanted to cheer him up."

"The Plum?"

"Yes, the Flowering Plum, the restaurant where I work. Haven't you been out on the East Side lately?"

"No."

"It's a swanky new place."

"What do you do there?"

"I'm a hostess. Sometimes I'm a cocktail waitress."

I shrugged. "I see."

Her eyes flashed blue sparks. "I don't think I like the way you shrugged. What did you mean by it?"

"Nothing," I said. "Now I see why you can drink beer at 11 in the morning, that's all."

"You're awful!" she said. "I don't like you at all. The Flowering Plum is a very nice Japanese restaurant. Sometimes I wear a kimono and I'm very demure and now I think I'll go home because I don't like you. The only reason I drank the beer was because Billy wanted me to and I didn't want to hurt his feelings."

"You're very kind-hearted," I said.

"You make me so mad!" She yanked her purse off the desk. "You're so suspicious. I'm going home!"

She strode through the doorway on those blue spike heels and as I watched her lovely to and fro motion, I knew I couldn't let her go away angry.

I caught up with her.

"I'm going out to 9 El Portal," I said. "Want to come along? I'll drive you home from there."

"No."

"Please accept my apology," I said. "I'm sorry if my questions embarrassed you."

She didn't reply, but trotted rapidly across the sidewalk, bouncing along on those high heels like a little fawn. I followed her.

"It's all my fault," I added, "but on the other hand I wouldn't have asked all those questions if you hadn't told me to be a detective. Anyway, don't you want to find out why poor little Felix was killed, shot down like a poor helpless creature in cold blood?"

That stopped her. She whirled around, eyes blazing.

"Yes, I do!" she exclaimed. "I certainly do! But I don't think a big, dumb ox like you will ever solve anything!"

I think she would have stood there the rest of the morning, but fortunately we were visited at that moment by an impetuous spring shower.

I grabbed her hand. "C'mon or you'll get soaked!"

We ran around the small stucco office building to my parking lot at the rear. We piled into my Chevy convertible.

"What about Billy?" she asked.

"He'll sleep it off."

"Aren't you going to put the top up?" She bent her head as two-bit-sized drops pelted us.

"No need to."

I yanked my raincoat off the back seat. There wasn't time, of course, to explain why I never drive with the top up. We both ducked cozily under the rain coat.

I drove with one arm around her, keeping it lightly in place across the back of her sky blue nylon sweater. These were definitely not ideal conditions for safe driving, especially the way the belt of the coat kept flopping in my eyes.

Then she noticed that the rain had stopped and she began to struggle out from under the coat.

Regretfully I let her go but the drive was practically over anyway, since we were now on El Portal Place, a one-block street which dead-ended at the beach. No. 9 was the last house. It was a California ranch house with long, slanting eaves and numerous windows. It was painted a brilliant mandarin orange with dove gray trim.

"You coming in with me?" I asked.

"No." She opened her purse and got out a jade-colored compact. "My hair's a mess, thanks to you."

"You look lovely," I said.

She was pleased and smiled at me. It was perhaps the

second or third time I'd seen her smile and I saw how
really beautiful she was.

"Don't go away," I said. "I'll be right back."

I went up the flagstone path to the house's main entrance, which faced the ocean instead of the street. I didn't
know what to expect. The only reason I was there was
because the card on which the initial S and the phone
number had been written had been so new and fresh. And
the handwriting had been so distinctly feminine it had intrigued me.

As I rang the bell I glanced in the window adjoining the
door but I couldn't see a thing because of the drapes.

I rang the bell again and then I heard a grunt.

I turned just in time to see a small man launch himself
at me from behind the acanthus bush near the porch.

He looked like a flying squirrel as he dived at my legs; I
was so fascinated by the sight of him—that I forgot to get out
of the way.

His aim was excellent. He knocked me flat. He scrambled
upright before I did and as I started to rise he walloped
me on the jaw with splendid accuracy. For a small man, he
had an immense fist. I fell back against the door and he hit
me again, in the eye this time, and I saw a beautiful Techni-
color burst of the northern lights. He swung a third time
but he was over-anxious and missed, and that gave me time
to leap to my feet.

It also gave me time to recognize him. He was King
Harold, the Filipino I had seen in the jail a couple of hours
previously.

"I'll teach you!" he shouted. "I'll teach you to come sniffing around!"

They didn't call that boy King Harold for nothing. He
was only a featherweight, standing maybe five feet three
or four, and he moved like a little helicopter. He flew in
under my defense, smacked me two or three times in the

abdomen with those big hands of his, and then skipped away, sneering at me. I tried to hit him but it was impossible because he was too small and too fast. He spun in close again, banged me in the belly, as he moved back I tried to hit him again.

I missed, of course. I saw then that this project was going to take a little extra doing. I moved away from the door out into the center of the broad porch. He began circling me, making me dizzy with his quick gyrations which he interrupted by ducking in close to hit me. He socked me each time in the same place in the belly and the monotony of it made me mad. I waited till he came around again and when his back was to the door I spread my arms and legs and advanced upon him the way you do when you're trying to capture a chicken in the barnyard.

He backed into the door and that's when I pounced.

He squawked when I folded my big arms around him. He squawked only once because I held him against my chest and calmly squeezed all the air out of him.

I squeezed him for about a minute and as I watched his expression change I decided he had one of the most ugly faces I'd ever seen. His nose was flat and the same dingy color as a 1927 penny. His eyes began to bulge out as he choked from lack of oxygen so I released him.

King Harold was definitely dethroned. I could have eased his fall, I suppose, but my eye hurt and my belly wasn't exactly comfortable. His knees buckled, his head hit the door with a satisfactory thump and he lay quietly on his back, displaying his gold fillings from incisors to rear molars.

I left him there and walked back to the car. Ti-lo took one look at my eye and erupted into laughter.

"You look like you'd been popped with a bottle of ink!"

"Very humorous." I opened the car door for her. "Would you kindly come with me and keep watch over a certain fallen warrior while I see if there's anybody inside the house?"

She followed me up the path and around the side of the house. King Harold was still lying where I'd left him.

Ti-lo gasped. "Why it's—"

I imagine I gasped a little too.

King Harold was still lying on his back in the same position. But now there was a difference—a big ivory-handled difference.

Somebody had slipped a knife into his heart.

I didn't have to look too far to see who that somebody was. I heard an automatic transmission mesh and glanced at the alley in time to see a car traveling rapidly in reverse.

It was a heliotrope-colored Buick. And before it vanished I caught a glimpse of the two men in the front seat.

I could've sworn one of them looked like Kreena.

CHAPTER VI

I SHOUTED AT THEM, more a shout of surprise than anything else. Then I sprinted back to the Chevy. When I started the engine, I saw that Ti-lo had followed me but she was too slow and I couldn't wait.

I drove in reverse because the dead-end street was too narrow to turn around in. My big Florsheim squashed the accelerator so flat the motor roared like a jet trying for a new low-level speed record.

I covered that block in four seconds flat and when I got to the intersection I turned the car around, using at the most one rear wheel. I shot down Ocean Boulevard looking for the entrance to the alley.

The entrance was easy to find, but the heliotrope-colored Buick was nowhere in sight. I glanced in both directions along

Ocean Boulevard but I still didn't catch a glimpse of anything which remotely resembled lavender. I drove slowly down the alley, looking in all the back yards, but I drew nothing but blanks.

I drove back to the end of El Portal and parked. Ti-lo was standing on the curb where I had left her. Her face was pale, especially around her eyes and mouth.

"I was afraid you weren't coming back." Her voice was small and frightened. "I didn't know what to do."

"Sorry," I said. "I thought one of them was Kreena and whenever I see that face I go a little nuts."

"Who is Kreena?" she asked. "What did he do to you?"

I got out of the car. "I'll tell you, but not now. Sometime when we've got a lot of time."

I started walking back to the entrance of the house, but this time she didn't follow me.

"Come on," I said. "He won't hurt you."

She shook her head. "I couldn't stand to look at him again."

"You know him?"

"Yes. He's one of Felix's friends—Harold Pablo. He's a cook at the Flowering Plum."

"Did you know he was in jail this morning? Implicated in the shooting of Felix?"

She shook her head. "Harold was?"

"He sure was." I started walking again. "I'll be right back. I want to look him over before I call the Johns."

"Wait," she said.

She walked up close to me and touched my arm.

"You fought with him, didn't you?"

I nodded and pointed at my eye. "I've got the Mickey Mouse to prove it."

"But you—" she faltered. Her face, looking up at me, displayed concern and uncertainty. "You didn't—"

"No, I didn't," I said quietly.

"I'm glad," she said. "I'm very glad."

I walked back to the entrance of the house and this time there was   no change in the situation. King Harold was still lying on his back, the ivory-handled knife was still in his chest and he was still very dead. Kneeling beside him, I saw that the weapon was a steak knife, the expensive kind that you might find in an expensive restaurant like the Flowering Plum.

I tried· the door to the house and as I expected it was locked. The house intrigued me. King Harold had been extremely interested in keeping me from going in, so interested he had attacked me. Therefore there must be something inside he didn't want me to see. I decided to go inside and take a look before the Johns arrived and tramped all over everything.

With a tin can I smashed a small section of a window at the rear of the house, opened it and entered. It was a moderately large place, paneled with handsome birch. It had a split-level living-room area, two bedrooms and two baths, and, except for the drapes, it was totally unfurnished. I made a quick tour, leaving the inside doors open behind me, moving so fast that I felt only a touch of the claustro heebie jeebies. I opened cabinets and closets and found nothing interesting except a lavender silk scarf hanging on a hook in the closet of the master bedroom. It was almost the same color as the heliotrope Buick and it was such a strong reminder of Kreena that I felt a surge of nervous energy. I balled it up and put it in my pocket.

As I exited through the window, I shook my head. I remembered the words King Harold had shouted as he started pummeling me: *I'll teach you to come sniffing around!* And yet there had been nothing in the house that required protection, nothing at all to provoke his assault on me.

I went back and knelt beside King Harold's body. Very carefully I hunted through the pockets of his avocado green trousers and suit coat. I found all the usual junk—billfold, change, keys, handkerchief. I examined the keys, found one which was familiar.

It was an oriental key with raised characters and the design of a fish-shaped kite with a cord that coiled gracefully all over the face of the key. From my pocket I drew the key I had palmed off Inspector Lowney's desk, the key that had been among Felix's personal effects.

When I compared them, they matched perfectly. I stuffed all the objects back into King Harold's pockets and then, on a hunch, I tried Felix's key in the front door.

It didn't fit. I examined the brass lock and the door, discovered some fresh scratches and decided it was entirely possible the lock had recently been changed.

I had dallied long enough. Crossing the street to a neighbor's house, I phoned the cop shop and informed Inspector Lowney that he had just lost his No. 1 suspect in the Felix Pia case.

Inspector Lowney did not accept the news gratefully.

"Stay where you are!" he ordered. "Have you touched anything?"

"I've touched everything," I said cheerfully. "I put King Harold in a box with some marigolds and mailed him to the cop shop."

He slammed the receiver so hard he must've knocked wires loose from L. A. to Cucamonga.

I walked back to the Chevy and sat on the front seat beside Ti-lo.

"You got any guesses?" I asked her. "Any idea who those guys are in the Buick?"

"No," she said. "And I don't want to know. I want to go home."

"Sorry," I said. "We can't leave until after Inspector Lowney's inquisition."

Within a couple of minutes a suburban radio car arrived

and two uniformed Johns got out and walked past us to the side of the house. Cars kept arriving every few minutes after that and before long El Portal was a splendid traffic jam involving several black and white patrol cars, a coroner's car, a group of press cars and finally an impressive black Oldsmobile which contained Inspector Lowney and some other detectives.

They shuttled busily back and forth between the cars and the house.

After making his initial survey, Inspector Lowney walked out to the Chevy and asked me a flock of questions. I gave him the information straight because despite his idiosyncracies, Lowney is a good pro cop who can shred a bad story with remarkable skill.

He waited until I finished and then lit a fresh cigarette and briskly puffed up a blue cloud that enveloped all of us.

"So you busted the window," he said. "That makes two for you today. You working for the glass manufacturers?"

"Nope," I said.

"And you mean to sit there," Lowney added, "and insist that during the minute you left King Harold somebody slipped a knife into him—and then escaped?"

"Yep," I said. "Escaped in a heliotrope-colored Buick."

"No kidding?" he scowled. "That same damn Buick?"

"Yep. Think your boys will ever find it?"

"They will — if there is such a Buick." Lowney pulled thoughtfully on his nose, making it even more pointed than usual. "I don't like your story, Pool. I ought to lock you up."

"But you won't," I said. "No motive—right?"

"For the time being," he said. "If I need one, I'll find one."

"Meanwhile, Inspector, I'd like to ask you a question. Why did you let King Harold out of the can?"

"So we could tail him, figuring he might lead us to the other characters in this case. Unfortunately—"

I finished the sentence for him. "But unfortunately he gave

your boys the old now-you-see-me-now-you-don't?"

Flushing, Lowney walked away from the car. Then he spun on his heel and glared at me.

"Stick around," he said. "That's an order. I'm not through with you, not by a long shot."

"I'm a vegetable," I replied. "I'll sit here till my roots twine around the drive shaft."

Lowney harrumphed angrily; spat tobacco fragments partly on the sidewalk and partly on his new shoes; swore and stomped off to the side of the house.

"I still want to go home," Ti-lo glanced at her watch. "It's after one and I've got to be to work by three."

"Sorry," I said. "As long as Lowney thinks we're a couple of murderers, we just have to sit and wait."

She frowned indignantly. "Don't say things like that."

"I was only kidding. I'll drive you home as soon as Lowney releases us, okay?"

"Thank you." She drew her bare legs up on the cushion and before she smoothed down her blue taffeta skirt I caught a worthwhile glimpse of a ruffled slip. She sat tailor-fashion, her expression serious. "While we wait, would you like to tell me about your Mr. Kreena?"

"I don't think so."

"Do you have to be coaxed?" She opened her purse and took out two sticks of gum. "Here, I'll bribe you."

We unwrapped the gum and began chewing.

"Well," she said.

"I still don't think so. Couldn't you whomp up a bigger bribe?"

"Maybe."

"What have you in mind?"

"I'll tell you after you recite your piece."

Wondering if she had any other motive beside friendly curiosity, I shrugged. I hated myself for doubting her, but I couldn't help it.

"Okay," I said. "There's not a terrific lot to it. I was a buck sergeant in the Korean War. I was in what we called a B-2 squad, a small outfit that sneaked across the lines at night to capture an enemy private or two and bring them back for questioning by the higher-ups. Attached to us was a corporal from the Filipino Army. Corporal Kreena. A mighty sharp poker player who could speak pretty good Korean as well as English. He was a dapper guy who wore a lavender scarf around the collar of his uniform. He went with us on our trips because he'd lived in Korea for a short while before the war and knew his way up and down the hills. On our last trip across, Corporal Kreena gave us a thrill-a-minute tour."

"What did he do?"

"He led us smack dab into a North Korean command post and before we knew it, we were surrounded by the enemy. He'd sold us out. I don't know how much per head he got for us, but from the way he grinned while that Chinese major paid him off, I'd say it was plenty. And it wasn't the first time he'd pulled that caper, or the last. Well, they stuck us in a prison somewhere north of the Yalu River. And because I was a tough guy who wouldn't cooperate or answer their questions, they jammed me in a hole in an old mine at the rear of the prison. There were iron bars on one end, leaving me in a space about the size of your grandmother's bustle. I was in here for fourteen months. Solitary."

Ti-lo shuddered. "How did you keep from going crazy?"

"Easy. I counted lice. In the winter I counted icicles. Of course, it was so dark I couldn't see them. I counted by feel. The guards were a nice, careless bunch. They were supposed to show up every second day with my tin can of rice and water, but most of the time they let three or four days go by."

"It's a wonder you didn't die." Ti-lo's eyes were filled

with what looked like genuine pain. "You must have suffered terribly."

"Some," I said. There was no need to make her turn pea green, so I skipped the other details.

"It wasn't too bad," I added, my voice displaying that casual tone of the big brave ex-soldier. "I did develop one thing, though, besides the itch from my 14,211 lice bites. Hatred. I developed a hatred for my guards. But a bigger hatred for Kreena. I guess my hatred for that little gentleman is still the biggest thing this side of Zamboanga. And I've been looking for him ever since the war because a doctor advised me to find him."

"A doctor did? Whatever for?"

"He was a VA doc in Frisco. A real savvy head-shrinker; he was a guy you could talk to. He said that I'd really developed a terrific fear of Kreena. Well, of course, I told him he was nuts, because I wasn't afraid of a little ape like Kreena. But he convinced me. He said if I could find Kreena, meet him face-to-face again, it might help cure me."

"Cure you from what?" Ti-lo asked solemnly.

"I've got a touch of claustrophobia. Can't stand being closed in. When I'm shut in a room for a little while I get a dumb sensation, like I'm nailed inside a cigar box or something. I go pretty wild sometimes. In fact I put on a circus."

She gave me an odd look and for a moment I thought I might have told her too much.

"So that accounts for it," she said thoughtfully.

"For what?"

"Why you kept opening the door to your office this morning."

"Oh, that. Sure."

She bit her lip. "I'm sorry I kept shutting it."

"Forget it. It was sort of fun."

For a moment we sat without speaking.

"Have you seen him since?" she asked. "Kreena, I mean."

I shook my head.

"You've looked?"

"Yes. Continually. That Frisco doc told me I had to face Kreena again. He felt that was the only way I'd get rid of my fears and maybe even my claustro. He even advised me to beat the hell out of Kreena. He used a lot of high-faluting words, but it all came down to finding Kreena. Therapy, he called it. Well, I've done plenty of looking."

"Haven't you had any luck at all?"

"Some. After the war I went back to U. N. headquarters in Korea and looked up the records of Kreena's Filipino Army unit. I traced him all the way back to Manila, but I was always one step too late. He'd been discharged. Honorably. When I heard that, I nearly flipped. I located a brother of his in a town near Lingayen and found out that he'd been the black sheep of the family. He'd dabbled in everything from stolen U. S. Army C-rations to bootlegging booze. Two months before, he'd hopped a ship for California. By that time I'd used up all my Army pay, so I returned to Frisco and took a job driving a cab and after about a year I got the only break I've had so far."

"You saw Kreena?"

"No, but I ran into an old buddy of mine who'd been in my battalion for a while and knew Kreena. He told me that a week before he'd seen a Filipino on the street in Long Beach. He swore it was Kreena. So I quit my job in Frisco and came to Long Beach and I've been here ever since. It's over four years now that I've been here doing bail-bond work."

"Why do you do it?" she said. "You must meet a lot of terrible people."

"Not so many. I like to get guys out of the lockup. It works sort of like AA—you know, one drunk helps himself by helping another drunk. Every time I get some guy out it makes me feel less cramped myself. And besides I've made a few good friends around the cop shop who help me keep an eye on the Filipino colony here. So I've been looking and hoping, but so far I haven't had another good break."

I leaned back against the cushion and stretched my arms.

"Well," I said, "I recited my piece. Now where's my bribe?"

"You're chewing it."

"No, you don't. You promised to whomp up something better."

"I did?" She smiled at me.

"I'm waiting."

"All right. Turn and look straight out through the windshield."

I did as I was told, but I watched her from the edge of my eye.

Kneeling on the seat, she leaned over and kissed my cheek.

Before she could draw away, I folded her inside my right arm, took a firm grip on her shoulders and planted a big one on her lips.

She had plenty of oomph in the hand she used to slap me.

"You've got your nerve! You grabbed me like Jack the Ripper!"

I grinned at her. "You know the old saying. 'When a lady doth protesteth too much, it's time—' "

I kissed her again, exactly on target despite her squirming. . . . I was just beginning to get my second wind when a shadow fell across the front seat.

Such a pointed shadow could belong only to one man.

"When you two get through wrestling," said Inspector Lowney, "would you be good enough to answer a couple of questions?"

Ti-lo fled to the other side of the seat and I got out a handkerchief.

"Fire away," I said.

"My questions are for the girl," Lowney said. "You *are*

Miss Ti-lo Sullivan, aren't you?"

Looking at him apprehensively, she nodded.

"You were engaged to the man who got killed in the jail, Felix Pia?"

She nodded again.

Lowney popped a new cigarette into his mouth and lit it. "One of my investigators just contacted King Harold Pablo's mother. Is it true that you were also engaged to him?"

I knew there must be a mistake.

I knew she wouldn't nod again.

But she did.

CHAPTER VII

INSPECTOR LOWNEY was very pleased with himself.

"You're quite the little honeybee, aren't you, miss? You flit from fiancé to fiancé—then both men get killed. Do you consider this simply a coincidence?"

Ti-lo did not meet his harsh gaze. Her eyes looked down at her small hands; there were touches of crimson across her high cheekbones.

"I'm sure she's got a good explanation," I said, although I couldn't for the life of me guess what it might be.

"You going to tell me about it?" Lowney demanded.

"Yes." Ti-lo tilted her chin at him proudly. "I have nothing to hide. I did it for both of them as favors."

Lowney snorted. "You seem to scatter your favors to all comers. Even rutabaga-puss Pool rates."

"Quit trying to crumb up her reputation," I said. "I took advantage. *I* kissed her . . . *She* didn't kiss me."

"That's not the way I saw it," Lowney said. "But it's not important. The important thing is, Miss Sullivan, why were you engaged to two Filipinos at the same time?"

"Not at the same time," Ti-lo said. "First I was engaged to Harold. Then to Felix. And the reason was very simple. Both of them were bachelors living at home. Felix lived with his sister, Harold with his mother. And Felix's sister and Harold's mother kept harping on the same thing, insisting that the men quit running around and keep more regular hours. Settle down. So when they said they were engaged, they didn't get scolded so much, don't you see?"

Inspector Lowney threw his cigarette away and lit a new one. "That's the craziest thing I ever heard of."

"I never intended to marry either one," Ti-lo said. "I became engaged simply as favors."

"What kind of a lamebrain do you take me for?" Lowney said. "That favors' routine is pretty—"

He didn't finish because Ti-lo hopped onto my lap, leaned across the car door and swatted Inspector Lowney's face so hard his cigarette was launched like a smoking missile.

"I don't like your insults!" Ti-lo jumped back to her former position. 'They *were* favors—nothing more!"

Inspector Lowney didn't reply.

He rubbed his chin, as he stared at his cigarette which lay smouldering halfway across the street.

"I could've warned you," I said. "Miss Sullivan has the finest temper west of Dublin and east of Hong Kong."

"Can't we leave?" Ti-lo asked. "I want to go home."

"Certainly."

I started the Chevy's engine, backed around the patrol car behind us, and we went in reverse down the street.

Ti-lo waved at Inspector Lowney who still hadn't moved.

"Goodbye," she called. "Goodbye, you dirty man!"

He finally reacted and yelled something at us but by then we were too far away to hear.

"That was a beautiful shot," I told her as we turned onto Ocean Boulevard. "And he deserved it. Sometimes Lowney feels so much like a cop he forgets people have other feelings."

"I shouldn't have done it," she said. "Can he make things pretty hard for me?"

I gave her what I hoped was a convincing grin. "Don't worry about him. He's an honest John and he'll only do his job."

We didn't talk any more until we reached her place, a small but modern apartment house on East Seventh.

"I won't kiss you goodbye," I said as she got out of the car. "It would only lead to bloodshed."

"You're so right." She gestured with her open palm.

She turned away from the car.

"Wait, Ti-lo," I said. "Tell me one more thing. There's no chance, is there, that you might be engaged to anyone else? A third guy, I mean?"

That was definitely a mistake. Her face turned red. She raised her purse angrily and I ducked, expecting to be pounded down through the floormat.

Instead she stamped away on those blue spike heels.

"I'll see you this evening," I called. "At the Plum."

She didn't reply, nor did she look back at me.

As I drove downtown toward the office, I thought a lot about Ti-lo and her two fiancés, but I gave considerably more thought to the brown face I'd glimpsed the second time in the heliotrope Buick. It might've been Kreena's . . . then it might not.

One thing I knew for sure. I was going to keep mixing into this crazy deal until I saw that face again.

I stopped at the corner store, bought some bologna, cheddar and a loaf of bread, and then drove to my one-car parking lot.

The office door was ajar, but when I walked in Billy was nowhere to be seen.

I opened up the bread and started making sandwiches.

I went over to the bathroom door, which was closed, and yelled.

"Hey, Billy. Lunch!"

My simple three-word statement provoked far more re-action than expected.

There was a lot of pounding on the inside of the door, plus numerous other noises, mixed in with Billy's wrathful cussing.

"Fer cryin' out loud, Lew! Lemme out!"

I tried the knob, but the door was locked.

"Where's the key?" I said.

"You got eyes! Find it!" he howled.

After five minutes of hunting, every minute punctuated with irate shouts and insults from the bathroom, I found the key in the bottom of the wastebasket.

When I unlocked the door, Billy came hoping out on his good leg, his other trouser leg flapping emptily. His face was fire-engine red with rage.

"I should punch yer face in!" he shouted. Where ye bin all day?"

He didn't give me a chance to reply.

"Foine way ye treat yer old buddy! Lettin' me be locked up fer hours like a blinkin' owl! And you—"

He sputtered even worse as he noticed the bread, Bologna and cheese.

"Ye dog ye! Sittin' there all this time fillin' yer big belly while I rotted in me cell!"

I gave him a shove backwards and he sat down abruptly on the divan.

"Cool off!" I said. "I just got here! Where the blazes is your leg?"

He started to tell me, but his anger broke out again and he nearly choked. He pointed toward the bathroom.

"In there!"

I went into the bathroom, but I couldn't find it.

"Ye big dummy!" Billy exploded. "In th' window!"

I glanced up at the small window near the ceiling and

saw part of the aluminum framework of his artificial leg. The window opened inward on hinges, held at the proper ventilation angle by two small chains. Billy's leg had been jammed in between the window and the sill. The bathroom is narrow and high; even if Billy'd jumped on his good leg he couldn't have reached the window.

If it had happened to someone else it might not have been very funny. But Billy is such an oddball that almost everything that happens to him has a touch of the ludicrous to it. I couldn't help laughing.

"Shut yer silly snickerin' face!" he yelled. An' fetch me leg."

I moved one of the office chairs into the bathroom, stood on it and got the leg down.

As he put it back on he didn't thank me, of course.

"Well," I said, "are you going to tell me what happened?"

"In good time, me lad. Wait'll I get some vitamins in me poor saggin' stomach."

He picked up one of the sandwiches I'd made and his fuzzy gray eyebrows cocked upward at a critical angle.

"Where's th' beer?"

"I didn't bring any. You had plenty this morning."

"Foine thing! Foine thing!" He took a big bite out of the sandwich and pretended to gag on it. "I'll choke, that's what I'll do, and I'll die right here before your eyes."

"Go ahead," I said. "It'll cut expenses."

He made another sour face, rummaged through the lower drawers in my desk and found an unopened can of beer.

He grinned at me. "Whin ye goin' to get the refriger—"

"Niver," I said.

I ate a sandwich and waited patiently while he ate his and finished the beer. Finally he decided he'd kept me in suspense long enough.

"Well, it was this way," he began. "This big seven-foot chinaman come in an'—"

"The truth, Billy," I said. "If what happened had anything to do with Ti-lo, you better stick to the facts or we won't be able to help her."

With the empty beer can, he made the sign of the cross on his chest.

"The truth, s' help me," he said. "This Chinaman was the biggest one ever I seen. He was at least six feet, one or two."

"Chinese?" I said, "or was he a Filipino?"

Billy spread his hands. Maybe he was a Filipino, though I niver seen a king-size one like that before. He had a little sawed-off runt with him. They was both what I'd call well-dressed and they was polite enough whin they come in."

"Did they give their names?"

"The big one did. Mr. Mackerel, he says his name is. Like in holy mackerel."

"You sure?"

"Sure an' I'm sure. Even left his card here someplace, he did."

Billy picked through the papers on my desk and then handed the card to me. There was a name on it but no other identification. The name was *Edward Macapagal*.

"Yeah," I said. "Well, what did Mr. Macapagal want?"

"He was wantin' to know where Ti-lo went whin she left here. I didn't like his uppity ways so I wouldn't tell him. So him an' th' sawed-off brown one begin talkin' tough and th' little fella jabbed me with his elbow. So, then I socked him a dandy on th' top of his hairless head, round and brown as a nut it was, an' thin they both piles into me. An' there fer a while things were lively. But thin th' big fella biffed me one across th' back o' me neck, a judo cut it must've bin, and down I goes like I was hit with a harp."

"You stayed down, I hope?"

"Me?" Billy was aghast. "McCorkell stay down? They tries to leave an' I chase 'em out on th' sidewalk. They

biffs me again an' drags me inside. I runs after 'em again
an' they biffs me again and drags me into th' bathroom and
takes off me leg and hangs it in th' window like a boomin'
bird in a cage. Fair insultin' it was!"

He shook his head in sympathy for himself, then removed
his woolly boola-boola cap and used it to dust off the lumpy
shoulders of his surplus Navy peajacket.

"Let's go get 'em, Lew!" He glared at me fiercely. "Let's
go knock the juice out of 'em!"

"Where'll we find them?" I turned Macapagal's card
over, but there was no address on the back either. "Did you
see what kind of a car they drove? A Buick maybe? Lavender?"

"Nope," Billy said. "It was a Lincoln. Long and yellow, it
was."

"And that's all they asked? They just wanted to know
where Ti-lo had gone?"

He pulled his cap down almost to his ears. "Let's go get
'em, Lew. Let's go!"

"We will," I said. "We will. But first I've got to have
time to think."

I sat in my best thinking position, leaning back in my
swivel chair. It was entirely possible that the mysterious Mr.
Macapagal and sidekick were the two men who had been
cutting all the fancy touches in the heliotrope-colored Buick.
But if they were, then their visit to my office was unnecessary
since they had been at the house where King Harold was
killed and therefore knew Ti-lo's whereabouts. If so, their
visit to my office was a dodge. If they were a legitimate pair,
however, then their visit involved something else—something
pretty important judging by the way they had lit into Billy.

I looked Macapagal up in the phone book and saw that
he had a home in the ritzy Virginia Country Club section
and a business address on the East Side. I wrote both phone
numbers down on his card and as I did so, I remembered

another card, one I'd seen earlier in the day. It was then I realized I'd goofed.

"Blast it," I said.

"Blast what?" Billy asked.

"That business card I spotted among Felix's stuff in the jail," I said. "I was so blasted interested in the writing some gal put on the back, and her initial S, that I forgot all about the name printed on the front."

"What name?" Billy said. "Somebody I oughta know?"

"The name of another Filipino," I said. "At least it sounds Filipino."

I wrote the name down on one of my own cards. *Charles Horondo*. And after it I wrote the descriptive language which had been on the card. *Business Opportunities Broker*.

"Brother," I said, "this thing is getting complicated!"

"Quit yer stallin'," Billy said. "Let's go kick th' scales off Mr. Mackerel!"

I frowned. "I don't know. I think we ought to look up Horondo first. He might have something to tell me about Felix. Something about that fight Felix was in last night."

"To Hades with Horondo!" Billy took off his cap and emphasized his words by swatting it against the desk. "Let's be gettin' our hooks into Mr. Mackerel!"

"Sorry," I said. "First Horondo, then Macapagal."

"Yer an idiot!" Billy snorted. "If brains was dynamite ye couldn't blow up a Kleenex."

CHAPTER VIII

I FOUND Charles Horondo's name in the phone book, dialed and made an appointment to see him in twenty minutes. Then Billy and I locked the office, piled into the Chevy and drove out Atlantic Avenue.

Horondo's place wasn't much to look at. It was half of an old bungalow-style home that had been converted into two offices. The chipped gold lettering on the front window identified him as a broker dealing in the sale of businesses. The office opposite dealt in real estate.

"Wait for me," I told Billy.

He pouted, taking my suggestion as a personal insult. To give him something to do I added: "Keep your eyeballs peeled for a lavender Buick."

As soon as I walked into Horondo's outer office I had a hunch I was moving in the right circles. His secretary was a Filipino, a squat middle-aged woman.

She scowled at the door, which I left open behind me.

I also left the second door open behind me as I strode into the inner-office. I walked up to the man seated at the desk and gave him a firm businessman's handshake.

"Good afternoon, Mr. Pool," he smiled. "You said on the phone you were interested in buying a barber shop."

"That is correct," I said.

"I have several listings. One moment."

As he opened an index file, I studied him thoroughly, from the gleaming stone on his ring finger to his maroon cravat. He was a Filipino and he was perhaps a couple of years older than me, in his early thirties. He was beyond a doubt the most obscenely fat man I'd ever seen.

The "suet" was in soft layers all over him; fat heaped upon fat, contained in an olive-colored, oily skin. His face was like a basketball: he had only one chin, but it covered enough territory so that he appeared to be neckless. His gray shantung suit was beautifully tailored, but it could not conceal the indecent, mammary-like bulges that protruded from his chest.

"Ah, here we are," Horondo announced, holding up several cards. "We have rather attractive prices on these."

I pretended to be interested until he mentioned the prices,

which ranged from $5,000 to $8,000 each.

"We can't go that high," I said, sounding disappointed. "My partner's putting up half the money. Maybe you know him—Mr. Pia?"

I had a good solid moment in which to watch his reaction to Felix's name. The fat on his face didn't ripple or quiver. The expression in his shiny black eyes remained the same.

He did, however, drop one of the index cards. Unfortunately he dropped it at the exact moment that his secretary slammed the inner office door shut, making it impossible for me to determine what had caused his plump finger to twitch—the crash of the door or Felix's name.

"You must excuse my secretary," Horondo said. "She is unhappy because I wouldn't give her the afternoon off to attend a barbecue at the church. What did you say your partner's name is?"

"Mr. Pia," I said.

This time there was a pleasant reaction, including a wide businessman's smile.

"Joseph Pia," he said. "Of course. So you haven't a thing to worry about, money-wise. With him as your partner, you can buy as many barber shops as you wish."

I shook my head. "Wrong Pia. My pal's name is Felix and all we've got between us is three thousand."

Horondo shrugged. "That's good enough for a start. I'm sure I can get you the right terms" He leaned forward confidentially. "Now about this shop out on Tenth Street. I know the owner and . . ."

He gave me the hard-sell. His voice droned on and on as he outlined the money-making features of the three-chair shop. I listened as long as I could, but it was a very cramped office and with the door closed I could feel the old whammy closing in on me again.

I stood up, my knees wobbly, and the walls came toward me soundless as if on greased tracks. Horondo went out of perspective, too. He suddenly appeared to be about nine feet tall and two inches wide.

"Sorry," I gulped. "I need a little . . . air."

I reeled backward, grabbed what I thought was the doorknob and yanked.

It was a doorknob all right, but it didn't open the door to the outer-office.

Instead several small packages fell on my head and in my bewilderment, mixed with nausea, I stumbled over a chair. Finally I found the right door and yanked it open.

I felt better, although not at the peak of physical fitness by any means. I looked back into the office and saw that the first door I'd opened led to a closet.

I squinted down at the packages on the floor, trying to get them into focus, and then I realized they were firecrackers.

"Sorry," I said. "Didn't know what I was—"

"Perfectly all right," Horondo said.

He came around from behind his desk, and stooped over the red and yellow packages. He grunted with the exertion of picking them up.

While he was occupied, I picked up a couple of the packages and slid them into my pants pocket.

I mopped my face with my handkerchief. "I'm going home and lie down. Must've been something I had for lunch."

He followed me to the front door, yakking all the way about the basketsful of money I could make if I closed the barber-shop deal in the next few days. He continued his pitch out on the sidewalk and then he walked around the Chevy and opened the door for me.

He was still yakking when I pulled away from the curb.

"Run fer ye life, men!" exclaimed Billy, glancing back over his shoulder. "Th' ellyphants is loose!"

"Shut up!" I said. "He'll hear you."

" 'Twas that a man?" Billy demanded.

"That," I said, " 'twas Mr. Horondo."

"Sure an' I guessed it. Ye do any good?"

I drew out the packages of firecrackers and dropped them in his lap. "What do you think?"

"Ah-hah," Billy said. "Ye figger he's th' joker that threw th' popper at th' office this mawrnin'?"

"Could be," I said. "Him or his pals."

Opening one of the red packages, Billy lit a firecracker with the dashboard lighter and tossed it from the car. It exploded in the street with a bang of approximately the same force as that which had been tossed from the heliotrope Buick. It didn't really prove anything about Horondo, of course, but it sure scared the hell out of the guy driving the truck directly behind us.

"Not bad," Billy said. "I think I'll be stickin' a couple down Mr. Mackerel's neck."

I parked at a gas station and phoned Macapagal's office number.

"He's not here," a secretary told me. "He just left for the restaurant."

"Which one?" I asked.

"His restaurant," she added. "The Flowering Plum out on Los Amigos Avenue."

"Thank you very much," I said.

Surprised and pleased, I grinned at Billy when I got back in the car.

"Not bad," I said. "Macapagal owns the Flowering Plum, the place where Ti-lo works. It's also the place where King Harold worked. Maybe I should've followed your hunch and looked him up first."

"I told ye so! I told ye so!" Billy bounced on the seat cushion. "C'mon, let's git rollin'."

It was shortly after five o'clock when we arrived at the Flowering Plum. I found a parking place in front of the broad main entrance and we both got out. It was a big expensive-looking place, Japanese in architecture. In the center of the entranceway grew a huge, plum tree; its branches were a mass of pink blossoms.

Billy led the way into the vestibule, a curved room painted pink and decorated with large mirrors. It was such a big joint, with plenty of open doors, that I didn't feel any claustro heebie jeebies.

As a hostess came toward us, I jabbed Billy in the ribs.

"Take your cap off," I hissed. "Button your shirt."

He glanced at me with disgust. "Quit yer complainin'. Ye ain't no blinkin' Beau Bummel yerself, y'know."

He was more or less right. The place was so swanky I wished I'd worn a suit and tie.

"Dinner or cocktails, gentlemen?" asked the hostess, an oriental woman in a kimono.

"We'd like to see Mr. Macapagal. We'll probably have dinner later."

"Eat here?" spouted Billy. "After what him an' his pal done to me? I'd sooner be eatin' fishheads down on the pier. I'd sooner—"

"Lead the way, ma'am," I said.

We followed her into a main dining room which was slightly smaller than the coliseum. There were scores of tables and booths, all of which were occupied since it was still early for dinner. The cocktail lounge, however, was full of customers. Along the wall nearest to us was a row of doors, at least a dozen of them, evenly spaced.

The hostess bowed toward the row of doors. "Mr. Macapagal is in No. 2," she said. She went to the second door, opened it, looked inside and said a few words. Then she walked back to us.

"He will see you in a few minutes." She gestured toward a long red velvet divan placed near the wall. "Please wait here."

She bowed once more and departed silently.

"Why ye takin' this kind o' guff?" demanded Billy as we

sat down. "We should be in there now apoundin' his big skull." ·

"Shut up," I told him pleasantly. "First we'll try the gentle approach. If that doesn't work, then we'll beat his brains in."

"The gintle what?" Billy sniffed. "Yer losin' yer marbles, Lew. S' help me, yer —"

I didn't blame him for knocking off the chatter.

Because the creation which strolled into the dining room at that moment was enough to stun a grandstand of people into silence.

She was a blonde. There are many species of blonde, of course, ranging from dyed to dishwater.

This one was a golden apricot blonde. Her hair was exceptionally long, drawn back in a single narrow loop which curved over her left shoulder.

"Praises be to dear St. Pat!" Billy said. "She's coming over!"

"Quiet," I said.

But he was right. She had turned and was walking directly toward us.

CHAPTER IX

SHE DID MORE than walk. She shimmered. She was extremely tall, maybe five-ten or so, and that was a lot of shimmer. She wore a tight-fitting metallic gold dress which glittered at each step. Her left shoulder was bare and the loop of golden hair artfully covered part of the exposed skin. By artfully I mean the loop permitted about an acre of upper bosom to show.

Billy jumped to his feet, coughing and wheezing the way he always does when he's emotionally upset.

I stayed where I was, preferring to appear unaffected by it all. But I didn't miss one sway of those hips.

"Pardon me," she said, "but do either of you happen to have a Franklin Delano on you?"

"A what?" I said.

She smiled. "A dime."

Billy's hand went into his pocket as if jet-propelled.

"I left home in such a hurry," she said. "I didn't bring enough change for the cigarette machine."

Billy had finally fumbled a dime out of his pocket and as he thrust it toward her I more or less accidentally knocked it out of his hand.

"Are you sure one Franklin Delano is enough?" I asked her.

She nodded and by that time I had dug a dime from my own pocket.

"Thank you," she said.

Billy came floundering up from the rug and she accepted his dime also.

"You're very kind," she added. "Both of you."

Billy just stood there and stared.

"Are you?" he blurted. "Are you a natural—"

He began coughing again.

"You'll have to excuse my friend," I said. "What he meant was will you join us for dinner?"

She rewarded me with a tiny dramatic frown. "I'm very sorry. I'm already waiting for someone."

Turning, she walked slowly away from us and the new view was also exceptional.

The hostess appeared silently at our side.

"Mr. Macapagal will see you now," she said.

I was still watching the action.

"Who is that tremendous woman?" I asked.

"She comes in nearly every night," the hostess said. "I believe she's a dentist's wife."

We continued to stare until Ti-lo strode into our line of vision. She glanced at the blonde and then at us.

"All right, you two," she said. "Pick your eyeballs up

from the rug."

I grinned at her.

"Mr. Macapagal's waiting for them," the hostess said.

"I'll take them in," Ti-lo said.

We followed her to the row of doors and I noticed for the first time that she wore an aquamarine-colored silk sheath dress. I also noticed that the dress was slit up the side, revealing a great deal of lovely nylon-clad limb.

She saw what I was looking at and made a face at me. "Is that all you do? Look at girls all the time?"

"Sometimes I do more than look," I said.

"I don't doubt it," she said. "Take off your shoes."

"Why, Ti-lo," I said, "you little hussy. Right here?"

She blushed beautifully. "This is a Tatami room. The guests don't wear their shoes. Put these on."

She handed Billy and me pairs of slippers which we put on. Then she rapped on the No. 2 door.

"Come in," said a heavy masculine voice.

She opened the door and I saw a man sitting inside on the floor beside a low table.

"That's him," Billy whispered. "That's fish face. Let's be gettin' him while he's on his backside!"

Macapagal was a Filipino, but he was definitely not Kreena. As we entered he rose to his feet to greet us. He was not seven feet tall as Billy had first said, but he was the most king-sized Oriental I'd ever seen. He was several inches taller than me, at least six feet two or three. He was well-dressed in a dark blue suit with matching tie and he was handsome.

He glanced at Billy and smiled. "I see you recovered from our little athletic exhibition this afternoon."

He had a deep voice and pronounced his words with the care of a graduate in college English.

"Sure an' that I did, sonny," Billy bristled. "And this time I got me a sidekick. One wrong peep out o' you, sonny, and he'll be stompin' those big fins off ye!"

Macapagal gave Billy a second smile, but this one was lofty and disdainful. "That won't be at all necessary, I'm sure. Will you gentlemen join us for a little chicken Sukiyaki?"

We seated ouselves on reed mats around the square table which was about six inches above floor level. As Macapagal sat, his long arm eased around Ti-lo, drawing her down close to him.

"I was very worried about Ti-lo," he said, looking at me. "The police told me she was at your office and when I went there this afternoon and she was gone I became quite upset. After what happened to Felix, I was very concerned that something might have befallen my little Manila chipmunk."

He kept his arm around her and now he gave her an extra squeeze.

I didn't appreciate his display of affection. Nor did I welcome the fact that Ti-lo made no attempt to escape from the encirclement of that long arm.

And at about the same time the old whammy hit me and I knew I should have had better sense than to let myself get shut inside a room that small. The walls came marching in on me and the butterflies on the nearest Shoji screen seemed to be alternately circling and dive-bombing my head.

Billy saw what was happening and helped be to my feet.

The door opened just before we got to it.

A Filipino bartender in a natty red jacket stuck his head in.

"Does one of you gentlemen own that blue Chevrolet?" he asked.

I nodded stupidly.

"It's blocking our passenger zone," he said. Would you be good enough to move it, sir?"

I nodded again and stumbled as Billy helped me out the door. I picked up my shoes and dropped onto the red velvet divan to put them on. I cursed Kreena for what he had done to me, cursed him for filling my head with a ridiculous fear that I couldn't control. I knew that what the Frisco doctor told me had to be right. If I could find Kreena and beat the hell out of him, it would get the bats and beetles out of my belfry. But at that moment the job seemed impossible. I had no real proof that Kreena was in Southern California. I'd thought I'd seen his face in the Buick earlier in the day, but it could have been wishful thinking brought on by my enormous desire to find him.

"C'mon, Lew, me boy," Billy said sympathetically. "Don't be lookin' so dragged down. Where's th' grin yer always wearin'?"

"I feel rotten," I said.

"It's a change o' scenery ye be needin'. An' until something better comes along why don't ye be a lookin' over there?"

I gazed where his forefinger pointed and saw that the tall blonde was being very active again. She was now seated on a pink-leather stool at the bar, which was located opposite the row of Tatami rooms.

"There's something about that dame that intrigues me," I said. "I'd like to see the guy she's waiting for."

"Intriguin', sure," Billy winked. "Ye mean ye don't think she's waitin' fer her dentist hubby?"

"Of course not. She's probably got a date with a basketball team and they'll spend the night making —" I cleared my throat "—baskets."

Billy grinned. "That's more like th' old Lew. I'm glad ye be feelin' better."

I noticed the bartender approaching and I finished tieing my shoelaces.

"I hate to keep bothering you, sir," he said, "but your car —"

"I'm on my way," I said.

I turned to Billy. "Go keep an eye on Macapagal. I didn't like the way he was sprawling all over Ti-lo."

"I'll squirm me way in between 'em," Billy said.

Walking out the entranceway to the sidewalk, I saw that I had indeed parked the convertible in a white-curbed passenger zone.

I climbed behind the wheel started the engine and began backing up.

And it was then I heard the fainting sizzling noise. It sounded like the burning fuse of a firecracker.

I glanced over my shoulder and from the corner of my eye saw something falling toward the car.

In the next fragment of a second, I was aware of half a dozen things simultaneously.

I saw that a second-story window was open in the restaurant directly above the car.

I saw the movement of a brown arm that had tossed the object. The upper part of the arm was covered by a lavender-colored sport sleeve.

I saw that the falling object was emphatically not a firecracker.

It was a square block of TNT and the spark-shooting fuse was so short it was invisible.

I bailed out of the convertible like an Olympic high-jumper.

I landed in the street on my fanny. I bounced to my feet and was sprinting beautifully until I skidded on a waxed bread wrapper that some idiot had left on the pavement.

I landed on my fanny again and at that moment I blessed the idiot who had dropped the bread wrapper because one of the car doors came spinning through the air, passing directly over me. If I had still been running, it would have sliced me up like meat loaf.

The concussion was enormous. I was less than a dozen feet from the car and the force of the explosion rolled me over and over. I was pelted with points of flying gravel and shattered glass. The breath whooshed from my lungs and I had the distinct sensation that someone was standing on my eardrums.

I could hear windows rattling up and down the avenue and I was reminded of a day in Hungnam when a granddaddy North Korean mortar shell had shattered every window for a block in all directions.

I sat up and looked at the second-story where I had seen the movement of the brown arm.

The glass was cracked and the man was no longer there.

I cursed him and then I remembered the rest of what I had seen during that first crazy instant.

The falling block of TNT had displayed a yellow label.

I had seen such a label before, on explosives and ammunition manufactured by the British.

And I knew that a lot of those explosives had been assigned to other U. N. units, including the Filipinos.

I let out a happy yell.

"Kreena!" I hollered. "Krenna!"

CHAPTER X

I didn't bother with the car. As I ran past I saw that the front seat was upended on the hood and the windshield had been blown off. I rushed into the vestibule, dodging through the excited traffic of waiters and busboys who were running outside to see what had happened.

Crossing the main dining room, I bounded up the pink-carpeted stairway to the second floor.

My objective, of course, was to intercept the man in the lavender sport shirt before he got downstairs. I had no way of knowing whether the man was Kreena or an assistant, since I had seen only his brown arm, but it was obvious that Kreena had chosen the TNT as one of the messier ways to get rid of me. It was exactly the kind of thing a man like him would do.

I ran along a hallway that led to the front of the restaurant and then through an open door to a large banquet room.

The room was empty and from the doorway I saw the cracked pane above the open window which told me I was in the right place.

I ran back down the hallway, opening the doors to a smaller banquet room and two offices.

I saw no one.

I followed the hallway to another stairway at the rear of the building.

At the bottom of the steps I pushed through two swinging doors and found myself in a large kitchen.

I gazed around swiftly. Shrimp bubbled in a deep fat frier, rice boiled in a great pot on a black range and two trout were frying in a black skillet.

But there wasn't a cook in the place.

I knew where they were. Hearing the explosion, the damn nincompoops had bustled out to the street to see what had happened, allowing the man in the lavender shirt to stroll through the kitchen unseen.

Knocking open the kitchen's rear door, I looked out onto a silent parking lot. Half a dozen cars were parked on the asphalt, but there was no movement of any kind.

The man in the lavender shirt had made a comfortable getaway, as easy as strolling through a park on Monday morning.

I went back to the deserted dining room and sat down on a pink leather stool at the bar. The bartenders were out front with the rest of the mob, of course, so I grabbed the first bottle of bourbon I could find and poured myself a long one.

There was one guy I definitely wanted to talk to — the bartender who had given me the message to move my car. I wanted to know *who* had given him the message. If it had been the man in the lavender shirt, then the bartender would be able to describe him for me and at least I'd know whether the guy was Kreena or not.

The other two bartenders returned, along with a flock of customers, busboys and waitresses in kimonos.

But my bartender was nowhere to be seen.

I finished the bourbon and walked through the vestibule toward the street.

On the front steps I was nearly bowled over by Billy.

"Yer alive!" he yelled.

He slapped me gleefully on the chest with both hands. "An' here I was thinkin' ye'd been blown to tatters!"

Abruptly his tone changed and he punched me hard in the stomach.

"Why, ye big ox!" he scolded. "Ye ain't even hurt! All the time I was worryin', ye was —" He leaned closely and sniffed. "Whiskey! While I was sufferin' fer ye, ye was in there blottin' up whiskey like a towel! An' fer me ye wouldn't even buy a can o' beer! Why, I'll kick yer big chin in! I'll —"

"Later, Billy," I said. "Where's Ti-lo? I've got to ask her something."

He gestured at the car's wreckage. "She was over there a minute ago. Pale as O'Leary's shroud, she was."

"And what about Macapagal? Was he still with you two when you heard the explosion?"

"Fish face?" Billy snorted. "Not him. He left right after yerself did. Ye think he's the one that done th' blowin' up?"

When I found Ti-lo I questioned her about the bartender who asked me to move my car.

"That was Oliver," she said. "He's a very hard-working boy."

"Let's go find him," I said. "I've got a few questions for hard-working Oliver."

We checked the whole first floor of the building, but we didn't catch a glimpse of Oliver's natty red jacket.

"How late's he supposed to work?" I asked.

"Till two a.m.," Ti-lo said.

We returned to the dining room, which was beginning to fill up with dinner guests and an assortment of police officers.

When Ti-lo and I started toward the stairway, John laid a large hand on my shoulder.

"Lowney's looking for you," he said. "Stick around."

I brushed his hand off my coat.

He grabbed a handful of my coat. "You're sticking, bud!"

"Okay, I'll stay," I said, hating myself. "Go find Oliver, Ti-lo."

She nodded and started up the steps.

As the John and I walked across the dining room to the booths, Inspector Lowney came in from the vestibule, leading a new pack of officers.

We met in the center of the dining room.

"I held him for you," said the John, making it sound as tough as if he'd just captured Al Capone, Roger Touhy and Mickey Cohen after a five-day gunfight.

"Excellent," said Lowney. Turning, he issued sharp commands to the others. "Spread out. Take statements from everybody."

He turned back to me. "I want a complete story from you. Everything, you understand?"

I nodded. "Let's sit down. I'm pooped."

We went to one of the soft, pink leather booths and I gave him the straight, unshellacked facts, adding nothing and leaving nothing out.

"As far as I'm concerned," I concluded, "the label on the TNT is all the link I need. It's obvious that Kreena brought the stuff from Korea. It's also obvious that he tried to blow me into stew-sized chunks."

Lowney lit a new cigarette from the butt of an old one and grimaced thoughtfully through the smoke.

"I don't buy it. In the first place, you've only seen snatches of this guy, nothing to prove conclusively that it's Kreena. In the second place, you've no motivation. *Why* would Kreena want to kill you? What did *you* ever do to him? The way I heard it, he's the guy that loused up *your* life, not vice versa."

I shook my head, but inside I had to admit to myself that Lowney was right. The motivation was not clear-cut.

"It must be tied up with the killings of Felix and King Harold," I said. "Kreena's involved. He's trying to get me out of the way because I'm involved too — and he knows that if I ever find him I'll come as close to killing him as I legally can."

"Kreena." Lowney spat a fragment of tobacco into his handkerchief. "Kreena, Kreena. Can't you think about anything else?"

"No," I said. "And I've got a good reason to —"

Without warning, Lowney cuffed me hard across the face. "Why'd you blow up your own car?" he demanded.

I swung on him but the John standing near the table grabbed my arm before the punch was halfway across the table. He wrestled me back to my seat.

"You damn idiot!" I yelled at Lowney. "What d'you think you're doing? Who do —"

"Psychology," Lowney grinned. "It's in all the books. In wrath a man will often reveal his true feelings. Now relax and listen to me."

"Relax?" I rubbed my stinging cheek.

"Shut up, loud mouth." Lowney was very pleased with himself. "You're clear. If you'd just sat there after that slap, I'd have doubted you. You reacted normally, so shut up and listen. While you've been busy messing up your day, we've been accomplishing things. For example, were you aware that King Harold was a cook here?"

"Of course," I said.

"Did you know that Felix was a bartender here?"

"Of —" I hesitated. I realized suddenly that I'd blown that one. I had been so busy with so many other leads all day that I'd never gotten around to asking Ti-lo that elementary question.

Lowney lit still another cigarette. "And I don't suppose you know what King Harold and Felix were fighting about last night, do you?"

"Nope," I said. ·

From his coat pocket Lowney dug a lavender-colored metal cylinder. "They battled over this."

He handed the small cylinder to me and I saw that it was a lipstick. It gave off an exotic perfume.

"Whose is it?" I asked.

"We'll find out." Lowney returned the lipstick to his pocket. "And now I'll tell you something else you don't know. We found the lavender Buick. It was abandoned down by the beach. And who do you suppose it was registered to?"

He was so eager to tell me, I felt like feigning disinterest but I couldn't. The Buick could be the keystone to the whole business.

"Clue me," I said.

"It was registered to Riki Tagsisi. Ever hear of him?"

I groaned. "Not another Filipino?"

"Right. And where do you suppose he works?"

It was too easy. "Here?"

"Right. He's another cook." Lowney puffed up a storm of blue smoke. "So that's the pattern. They all work at the Flowering Plum — Felix, King Harold, Riki Tagsisi and that little friend of yours, Ti-lo."

"Complete the pattern," I said. "Why don't you tell me Ti-lo is enaged to Riki Tagsisi?"

"We haven't checked Riki out yet," Lowney said. "We switched signals when we heard about the big bang out here." He gestured to the John. "Go back to the kitchen and see if Riki Tagsisi is on duty."

The John departed and I completed a little more constructive thinking.

"Here's two more for your list," I said, "and again they both tie in with the Flowering Plum. One, find the owner, a tall drink of coconut juice who calls himself Macapagal. Find out where in the hell he was when the TNT went off. Two, find a blonde. She went out of her way to talk to me before the blast and I think she put the finger on me."

"What's her name?"

"It shouldn't be too hard to find out." I flagged down one of the bartenders.

"D'you know her name?" I asked him. The blonde who was at the bar?"

"Sure," he grinned. "Everybody knows her. Her name's Agnes."

I screwed up my face. "Agnes? Are you sure? What's her last name?"

"That's all we know her by." He shrugged. "Agnes."

"Have you seen her since the blast?"

He scratched his nose. "I don't think so."

"What about Macapagal? Have you seen him since the blast?"

"Yes. I saw him talking to Ti-lo."

"Thanks." I looked at Lowney. "You want to ask him any questions?"

"Not right now," Lowney said.

The bartender started to walk away.

"Wait," I said. "I nearly forgot. Have you seen Oliver since the blast?"

The bartender shrugged. "Not since I saw him talking to you."

"Okay. Thanks."

He walked away and I turned back to Lowney. "Oliver's another name for your list. He's one of the bartenders, the

one that told me to move my car. He might not be involved
at all, but I'd sure like to find out who told him to tell me to
move it, just in case whoever did it is planning another TNT
surprise for me. I might wind up with a permanent headache
next time."

"You have my sympathy," Lowney said. "Meanwhile I'll
trade for one more piece of information."

"You'll trade? What for?"

"You haven't told me everything. Right?"

He grinned the kind of grin that says I'm your friend, but
if you don't play ball I'll be the worst enemy you ever had.

"Give me a hint," I said. "What are you offering?"

"It might be a link to Kreena."

"Okay," I said. "I'll trade. I've noticed that heliotrope is
the only consistent item in everything that's happened. The
Buick was lavender-colored, and so's that lipstick you found.
And the guy who tossed the TNT at me had on a lavender
shirt."

"No kidding?"

"No kidding. And check this." From my coat pocket I
drew out the lavender scarf. "This is object No. 4 on the
heliotrope parade — the same color scarf Kreena wore on
his uniform in Korea."

Lowney took the scarf from my hand and sniffed it.
"Where'd you get it?"

"It was in a closet in that house on El Portal. The house
where King Harold was knifed."

"Mind if I keep it?"

"Go ahead. And now what about your end of the trade?"

"Right." Lowney grinned again.

"I've seen the medical examiner's report on Felix," he said.
"Would you be fascinated if I told you Felix had plastic
surgery done on his face a few years ago?"

He was right.

I was fascinated.

And at that moment, I could think of only one person who might want to change his face.

CHAPTER XI

The moment didn't last long enough. I had scarcely started turning the reasons over in my mind when Billy dashed down the pink stairway and over to our booth.

"'Tis a calamity!" he gasped. "By all that's holy, 'tis —"

He was out of breath. He was also at least fifty percent drunk.

His face was white as an eggshell, a sharp departure from its normal shade of tile red.

"I'll show ye!" He pointed at the top of the stairway. "C'mon!"

He went up the stairs ahead of us.

Midway along the second-floor hallway, he halted and pointed a shaking finger into the open doorway of one of the executive offices.

I looked in and saw Ti-lo lying on her back on the floor; I saw bloodstains on the bodice of her dress and then I saw the knife in her hand and I was filled with dread.

Lowney and I knelt together beside her and I picked up her other hand and touched her quiet wrist.

I held my breath.

Then I realized I was pressing too hard and as soon as I relaxed my fingers a little, I felt the beat of her pulse.

"She's alive!" I said.

"Thank the great foine lord!" Billy crossed himself. "An' what about him?"

"Him?" Lowney said.

"Behind th' desk," Billy said. "His eyes be lookin' upward like two sad nails in a board."

Lowney and I stepped carefully around Ti-lo and saw a man lying under the window.

Somehow the fact that it was Oliver, the bartender, didn't surprise me at all. I didn't have to touch his wrist to tell there was no pulse. The waxy tan color of his face, the sightless film across his eyes and the mouth, twisted open — these were enough.

"I don't believe she could do such a thing."

Then Lowney had quite a time producing all the motions and noises of the professional cop at work. He spent a lengthy minute examining the way her fingers were bent around the handle of the knife, and I noticed then that it was an ivory-handled steak knife, identical to the one which had pierced King Harold's heart.

Several minutes dragged past while Lowney crept on his hands and knees to a point on the floor midway between Oliver and Ti-lo. He studied the wound in Oliver's chest, the red stains on the floor and the other stains on Ti-lo's and then he shook his head slowly and thoughtfully.

"It's too bad," he said. "Sure too bad." He glanced at me. "Okay, revive her."

I lifted both her arms, shook the knife from her limp fingers and began by massaging her wrists. Then I propped her legs up on the rungs of a chair, keeping her skirt carefully in place, to the disappointment of the crowd of Johns and waiters jammed elbow-to-elbow in the doorway. I pinched her cheeks gently.

"Ti-lo," I said quietly. "Ti-lo . . ."

Her shadowy eyelids slipped open a little at a time. And then her large eyes were looking up at me, fully open, and they were the most innocent blue I've ever seen.

"Lew . . ." It was the first time I'd heard her speak my first name. "What are you —"

Turning her head, she saw the blood and the knife and she began to scream.

I picked her up. The jam of Johns and waiters parted and I carried her to the adjacent office, lowering her onto a chair. By this time she had begun to cry.

"Go ahead," I said. "Have a good wet one."

She didn't cry very long. She dried her cheeks with a corner of my handkerchief.

"Thank you, L-Lew," she said. "V-very much." She managed a small smile and then Lowney came in.

"All right," he said, crisply business-like. "I'll need a few answers from you, Miss Sullivan. Now take your time, try to relax and tell me exactly how it happened."

Her lips quivered. "I w-went — I went looking for Oliver, because —" She glanced at me. "Because you wanted to talk to him. I was in the hall when I heard him cry out the first time, in such pain, and I — I went back to the office. I saw that I hadn't noticed him before because he was behind the desk. When he saw me, he cried out again. I'll — I'll never forget what he said. He —"

Closing her eyes, she bowed forward in the chair, bending so low her forehead touched her clasped hands which rested on her knees.

"What did he say?" Lowney asked.

Ti-lo raised her head and her eyes were wet with fresh tears.

"Let me finish," she said. "T-there's very little more. He cried, 'Take it out!' I told him I'd get a doctor and he screamed, 'No, take it out! It's killing me!' I couldn't stand the thought of touching it, but I — I forced myself. I pulled and it came out so — easily, and then, before I fainted, he said one more thing. He said —"

She closed her eyes.

"Out with it," Lowney bent his head close to hers. "What did he say?"

Her voice fell to a whisper. "One word, one last word. He said 'Thanks . . .' "

For a moment, Lowney was silent. He snapped his lighter, lit a new cigarette and scowled down at her.

"I knew it," he said. "I knew you'd say you pulled the knife out. That's what they always say. And, of course, you haven't a witness, have you? No one saw you pull the knife out?"

Ti-lo shook her head.

I put my hand on Lowney's shoulder and dragged him away from her.

"You're crazy to doubt her," I said. "There's a batch of others involved in this thing and they look twice as guilty as her. They've all got —"

Lowney cut me off sharply. "Name one. Name me just one!"

"Macapagal!" I said. "The owner of this place. All the dead people in this deal are his employees. All three of them. As for motive, that's not hard to find either."

I strode over to Ti-lo's chair. "What's Macapagal to you? I saw him put his arm around you."

Her eyes looked up at mine without faltering. "He says he's in love with me."

"Do you love him?"

"No."

"Could he have been jealous of Felix and King Harold because you were engaged to them?"

She shook her head, "I don't know."

"What about Oliver? Was he in love with you?"

"I don't know." She paused. "I don't think so."

"Macapagal might've thought he was," I said. "You never know what a jealous guy will think or do."

I hadn't realized Macapagal was standing in the open doorway just behind the Johns and waiters and had overheard me.

He strode into the office and confronted me. There was dignity on his long dark Filipino face, enough dignity for half a dozen congressmen, and his black eyes were brilliant with anger.

"You hurt me deeply, sir!" His voice had a unique deep resonance, like a cannon fired in a cathedral. "Your charges against me are extreme nonsense!"

"Are you in love with Ti-lo?" I demanded.

He nodded toward her. "I have a great affection for Ti-lo."

"Where were you when the TNT exploded?"

It seemed to me that his shiny black eyes wavered. But his voice boomed with authority. "Sir, your implication is distressing! I was making a phone call at the time of the explosion!"

"You can prove that, of course?"

"Unfortunately, sir, I cannot. The line was busy but —"

"Knock it off!" interrupted Lowney. "For crying out loud, since when are bail bondsmen in charge of Police Department interrogation!"

He prodded the sharp nail of his forefinger against my chest.

"Out, Pool!" he ordered, jabbing me a second and third time. "Out! And don't come back till I send for you!"

He pushed me out the door and then slammed it.

I walked immediately to the door of the other office and rapped it with my knuckles.

A sourpuss John opened it.

"What d'you want?"

I brushed past him. Lowney says it's okay for me to look at the stuff you got out of Oliver's pockets."

He didn't try to stop me. I walked to the desk and looked at the objects collected there. I looked for a key of oriental design, like those which had been among Felix's and King Harold's effects, but there was none. The objects were routine — except for a white business card.

Bending closer, I read the writing on the card. "Wed. S." There was also a phone number and I recognized it. It was the same one I'd memorized off the card which had been in Felix's pocket. And the feminine writing was the same.

I gave the card a quick flip, exposing its other side. I saw five words I quickly recognized: *Charles Horondo, Business Opportunities Broker.*

Having seen quite enough, I left.

Out in the hall I met a lot of traffic moving from the other office. In the middle of the mob was Lowney and I saw that his left wrist was handcuffed to Ti-lo's.

"Don't you say a word," he warned. "I'm taking her in and that's that."

You've got an answer for everything," I said. "So what was her motive, answer me that!"

"Out of the way!" Lowney shouldered past me. "I'm holding her on suspicion of murder. I'll find the motive!"

I followed them along the hallway. At the stairway, Billy joined the parade and we walked across the dining room and out to one of the black police cars parked in front of the restaurant.

Lowney and Ti-lo sat in the back. Ti-lo hunched down, looking smaller than ever. All I could see were her eyes and they were the frightened eyes of a rabbit surrounded by gun muzzles.

"I didn't!" she cried as the car pulled away. "I didn't do it!"

I stood with Billy and watched the ruby tail-lights vanish around the corner.

The thought of Ti-lo sitting in a cell behind gray-painted bars made me ill. Even though I was standing outside on the sidewalk, I felt the old whammy of bars and walls marching in on me.

I shuddered.

I had to get her out. And the sooner I did it, the better it would be for both of us.

Billy and I hailed a cab. We rode for a few minutes, then stopped near a drugstore on Tenth Street and while the cab waited we went to a phone inside.

"Who you callin'?" Billy asked.

"I want to talk to Riki Tagsisi," I said. "Lowney got so worked up over Ti-lo he never did talk to Riki." I put my hand over the mouthpiece and lowered my voice. "Riki owns the lavender Buick. I want to find out if he was driving it."

Billy nodded wisely.

The Flowering Plum's phone was answered by one of the hostesses.

"Mr. Tagsisi," I said.

"Who's calling?" she asked.

"Police Department," I said. "Inspector Lowney."

"Oh." She paused. "I'm sorry but Mr. Tagsisi left early tonight."

"Then give me his address."

"One moment please, sir."

I waited.

"Sorry, sir," she said. "His address isn't listed in our personnel records. Would you like to talk to Mr. Macapagal?"

"That won't be necessary," I said. "Thank you."

I put another dime into the phone and dialed Sergeant Phister, the night shift booking sergeant at the cop shop. I asked him to do me a favor and see if he could get Riki Tagsisi's address from the boys in Lowney's department.

"I'll phone you back," he said.

While we waited, we invited our hack driver inside and we had coffee and hamburgers together at the drugstore counter. When we were nearly finished, the phone rang.

"No go," Sergeant Phister said. "Lowney's boys leveled with me and they said they've been trying for a couple of hours but still haven't located Riki's address."

"Thanks, sarge," I said. "I owe you a box of Roi-Tans for a good try. And I'll give you another box if you can get me the address of Felix Pia, the little guy who was shot this morning in one of your suites."

"I'll phone you back," Phister said.

In less than a minute the phone rang.

"That one was easy," Phister said. "It's 1214½ Daisy. He lived there with his sister."

"You're a good kid," I said. "The two boxes will be on your desk tomorrow night."

"I'm trying for three." Phister chuckled good-naturedly. "Call me back in an hour and maybe I'll have Riki's address."

"Don't be a piker, sarge," I said. "Try for four. Lowney'll be bringing a girl in pretty soon, a nice little doll named Ti-lo Sullivan. How about telling the matrons to give her a break and treat her gently?"

"Four it is," Phister said. "They'll treat her like she's the chief's best gal friend."

We hung up. It was all a gag, of course, about the four boxes. Sergeant Phister is a good cop, a happy man who likes his work, and we've been wisecracking buddies ever since we were introduced by Winebrenner, the dayside booking sarge. I made a mental note to get Phister six cigars. He would consider any more than that a bribe and an insult.

Billy and I got back into the cab and the driver took us downtown to a rent-a-car agency on American Avenue. I rented a black Ford which looked, at first glance, like an official city car. I rolled all four windows down, trying to kid myself into believing I was in a convertible, and we drove out to the address on Daisy Avenue.

I walked across the sidewalk to Felix's place, a ground-level flat in a sagging stucco building that had been needing repairs for at least ten years.

My knock on the door was answered by a sad-eyed, thirtyish woman in a yellow housecoat.

"Hello," I said. "You're Felix's sister?"

She nodded. "Are you another one from the police?"

"No," I said. "I'm a friend of Ti-lo's and I'd like to ask a couple of questions. May I come in?"

We walked into a shabbily furnished living room and sat down. The room was very small and I wished she'd left the front door open, but it couldn't be helped.

"I know you'd rather not talk about it," I said, "so I'll be as brief as possible."

"Thank you." She touched a small wrinkled handkerchief to her eyes. "Felix did a lot of wild running around, but he didn't deserve what happened."

"Neither did the others," I said. "King Harold and Oliver."

She raised her head and her eyes were unbelieving. "Oliver too?"

"Probably by the same person," I said. "And you can help, if you feel up to it. I want you to tell me anything about Felix's behavior in recent weeks that was odd. Can you think of anything?"

She bit her lower lip. "Well, I suppose there were a few things."

"Go ahead," I said. "I'll keep it confidential."

"Well, the worst one was the way Felix never had any money. He had a good job as bartender, made over one hundred dollars a week and he never had any money. He was always borrowing from me and I make less than sixty, take-home."

"Do you have any idea where Felix was spending his money?"

"No. I'd ask but he'd never tell me."

"What else was odd about what he was doing?"

"Just one thing, I guess. He never came home on Tuesday nights."

"You mean not at all?"

"That's right. Week after week it was always the same. He never came home Tuesday nights and he'd never tell me where he went."

"Did he gamble? Do you think he was spending the night rolling dice somewhere?"

She shook her head. "Felix never gambled. He said gambling was for fools."

I thought over what she'd said and then I got up from the divan and took a few steps around the room. I eyed the closed front door, but I decided I could take it for a few more minutes.

"I've got three more questions," I said, "and then I'll be on my way. One, did you ever hear Felix mention a man by the name of Kreena?"

She shook her head.

"Two," I said. "Do you know why Ti-lo and Felix got engaged although they weren't supposed to be in love?"

"That one I can answer," she said. "He didn't kid me. He was trying to make me think he was starting to settle down."

"Three." I paused because this was perhaps the most important one and I didn't want to louse it up. "Why did Felix have plastic surgery done on his face?"

"Well," she said, "there was nothing odd about it. He was badly cut up in an auto accident and they had to repair his face."

"How long ago did it happen?"

"About five years ago."

"I goofed," I said. "I've got a fourth question and this is definitely the last. Have you any pictures of Felix taken before his accident?"

"No."

I gave her an even more electric smile, a real battery-burner, and I spoke two quick blunt words.

"You're lying."

It worked.

Her eyes widened and her lips twitched.

"Show me the picture," I said. "I promise not to tell anyone you've got it."

Rising slowly from her chair, she looked at me in open wonder.

"How did you know?" she said.

I didn't have the heart to tell her.

"Some other time," I said.

"I didn't lie to the police," she said. "I forgot there ever was a picture, Felix had so few taken. After they'd gone, I remembered. And when you asked, I thought I'd better —"

"Let me see it," I said.

She went into another room and came back with a thick Spanish-American dictionary. She riffled the pages and a snapshot fell to the floor.

I picked it up.

It was a picture of five men, all Filipinos in sport shirts and slacks, standing in front of a DeSoto.

I felt a sudden surge of excitement.

The face of the man in the middle was the same face I'd seen grinning the night he accepted the money for selling me and my squad to the North Koreans.

It was Kreena, all right.

CHAPTER XII

FELIX's sister stepped closer and placed a red, work-worn finger on the snapshot.

"That's him," she said. "That's Felix on the left there."

I dropped onto a chair and stared at the picture, I examined the figure on the left, comparing it with my memory of the man I'd seen in the icebox at Clapper's mortuary. The plastic surgery hadn't changed Felix's face a great deal. The mouth was different, the cheek-line was changed, but the hairline and ears were the same, and the general Virgil Partch-proportions were definitely Felix's.

"Who's this guy?" I pointed to Kreena. "This poisonous-looking character?"

She leaned over my shoulder. "I've never seen him. He never came around, but I know all the others. There's Oliver and King Harold and Riki."

She was indeed right. And I had also met them all. All except Riki.

I put my finger on him. "This is Riki Tagsisi, I presume?"

"Yes, that's Riki, a very polite boy." She sighed. "They had sort of a club, you know. The Five Manilas, they called themselves, because they were all born in Manila but raised in this country. They went hunting together and fishing and to the bullfights in Tijuana." She sighed again. "And now three of them are dead. It's so hard to believe."

I put my finger on Kreena's face. "Didn't you think it was odd that this guy never came around, that you never got to meet him? Did Felix ever mention his name?"

"Carlos? Sure, he mentioned Carlos all the time."

"Did he ever mention Carlos' last name?"

Her forehead wrinkled thoughtfully. "He might have, but I've got a good memory and I would've remembered if he had. No, I don't think he ever did."

"Thanks," I said.

I sat on that hard, wooden-backed chair staring at the picture. I felt better, much better, now that I knew Kreena was still alive and very much involved in all three killings, because that meant I still had a chance to beat hell out of him. But I was now more bewildered than I'd been before. My head was jammed with circles of confusion. What I needed was a link, evidence which would link Kreena directly to Macapagal. Then my chances of getting Ti-lo out of the lockup would improve 10,000 percent.

But what in the bloody blue blazes was the link?

I sat there staring at the snapshot, feeling shut-in and lousy. The more I stared at the snapshot the more confused I got. I wondered why I was so certain that Kreena and Macapagal were the evil angels. Why couldn't there be a link between Kreena and Horondo, the human blimp whose business cards had showed up in the pockets of the dead men?

Furthermore, who was S, the lady whose phone numbers showed up on the back of the cards?

I glanced at my watch. It was nearly ten and I'd stayed much longer than I'd intended. But I didn't want to leave yet. Despite those persistent expanding circles of confusion, I felt that I was close to arriving at something significant. I ran the facts through my brain again, efficiently this time.

And then it hit me. I had mentioned it a few minutes before in my conversation with Falix's sister.

The link had to be Riki Tagsisi!

And he was undoubtedly next on the list of victims. Three out of five in the picture were already dead. The pattern indicated there might soon be a victim No. 4 and a No. 5.

A No. 5?

I came up from the chair so fast Felix's sister slipped in surprise from her perch on the arm of the divan.

"Is something the matter?" she said.

I didn't reply. I was thinking about the pattern. If all the men in the picture were marked for extinction, that meant Kreena's number was up, too.

And I couldn't stand for that. If anybody was going to put Kreena's number up, it had to be me.

I looked around the living room. "Where's your phone?"

"In the kitchen," she said.

After two tries I dialed the right number for the cop shop and talked to Sergeant Phister.

"How're you doing?" I said. "You got Riki Tagsisi's address yet?"

"Nope. Sorry, Lew, but Lowney's boys tell me Riki moves from apartment to apartment faster than a Fuller Brush man."

"What kind of a mood is Lowney in?"

"Ratty," Phister said. "I wouldn't bother him if I was you."

"Thanks, sarge, but I'll have to try."

I dialed again. As soon as he heard my voice, Lowney crackled the lines with profanity and hung up on me.

I was in no mood to be upset by a little unpleasantness. I dialed again.

This time I hit him with a blast of profanity first and while he listened, stunned into temporary respect, I added:

"Don't you realize Riki Tagsisi will be the next one?"

"What makes you tnink so?"

I told him about the picture and that fact that all three dead men were on it, plus Riki Tagsisi and Kreena.

He was impressed, but he tried to keep it a secret.

"You sure your imagination hasn't blown another gasket?"

"You're full of official heifer dust," I informed him calmly. "The picture proves once and for all that Kreena's in this deal. And only something important, something big and lucrative, would bring him here. I've already told you only two guys in the snapshot are still alive, two guys in their club known as The Five Manilas. The next step will —"

"Wait a minute," Lowney said. "Let me write that down. The Five Manilas, did you say?"

"Right. And if we don't get moving, Kreena will kill Riki or Riki will kill Kreena — or somebody else will knock off both of them." I'd tried everything from profanity to insults and now I let my voice drop to a friendly wheedling tone. "Look, Inspector, I've traded information to you all day. Now for crying out loud why don't you tell me what you've got on Riki Tagsisi?"

For a moment Lowney's end of the phone was silent except for the sound of other Johns babbling in the background.

"All right, Pool," he said. "Maybe I've been too rough on you. We've found out that Riki left the Flowering Plum a few minutes after the TNT was tossed at your car. He left with a woman."

"A tall blonde?"

"Right. We found out her name is Agnes Sweet."

A switch clicked in my brain. The feminine initial on

the back of Horondo's cards was S. It could very well be S
for Sweet.

"Excellent," I said. "Did you confirm that she's a dentist's
wife?"

"That part didn't check out. She's spread propaganda about
being a dentist's wife, but we don't think she is."

"You got an address for her?"

"Nope. She and Riki have dropped completely out of
sight."

We paused while I thought that over and I could tell
Lowney was within a whisper of hanging up on me again.

"What about Ti-lo?" I said. "How much do I have to raise
to spring her?"

"Forget it," he said. "You'd need at least five thousand and
I happen to know you haven't got enough lettuce to spring
a hamster. See you around, Pool."

He hung up on me again, but I didn't mind. You can get
used to anything.

I stood there in the kitchen for a few moments, feeling tired
and rundown. And at the moment I didn't have one fresh
idea on how to get Ti-lo released. I wondered what had
happened to all the progress I thought I'd made; suddenly
it all seemed to have slipped down the drain.

You know how it is, though. Just when the clouds are
darkest, that's when the silver lining drops down and thumps
you on the head.

The thump in this case was a voice.

A woman's voice with sexy undertones. It was definitely
not the voice of Felix's sister.

Leaving the kitchen. I kittyfooted through the dining room
and managed a one-eyed peek into the living room.

The woman standing there talking to Felix's sister was the
tall blonde!

"I was wondering," I heard the blonde say, "if you could
do me a favor. I lost a key the other evening at the Flowering

Plum and Felix was going to return it to me. Did he mention it to you, by any chance?"

"No, he didn't."

"It's an unusual key. It fits an antique desk in the library at my home. My husband — he's a dentist — you know — collects Chinese *objets d'art.*"

"No, I'm sorry. Felix never mentioned it."

That was my cue.

"Is this the object you mean?" I said.

From my pocket I drew the oriental key that I had sneaked off Lowney's desk.

The blonde awarded me a sunny smile.

"Well, hello again," she said. "It's so nice to see you."

"And it's so nice to see you," I said.

My statement was all fact. Since I'd seen her last, she'd changed clothes. She now wore black ballet slippers, black Capri pants that fitted as snug as my glance and a black shirt which was deliberately left unbuttoned almost to her navel. I noticed that part of a lavender bra was visible under the coil of hair. Since I was so preoccupied she found it easy to slip the key from my fingers.

"Hey!" I said.

"Thank you very much." She held the key between two long, mother-of-pearl painted fingernails and examined it. "Yes, I do believe this belongs to my husband's desk."

I reached out quickly and plucked it away from her.

"Now it's my turn to say thank you," I grinned. "I'd be glad to give you the key, but it's not mine to give."

With noticeable distress, her golden brown eyes watched my hand place the key in my pocket.

"It's not?" she smiled. "Wouldn't you like to discuss it a little further, say over a drink somewhere?"

"Let's," I said.

CHAPTER XIII

I THANKED Felix's sister for her help and accompanied the blonde down the front steps and out to the sidewalk. There was a Buick parked behind my rented Ford and enough light shone on it from the corner delicatessen to indicate its color.

It was more than slightly familiar.

It was heliotrope.

I gestured at it casually. "Your car?"

She smiled. "Uh-huh. Shall we go in it?"

"Sure," I said.

My brain was doing athletic flip-flops which I hoped didn't show. The Johns had impounded a lavender Buick which they'd found abandoned at the beach — and yet here, big and sassy, was an identical model. It had to be a duplicate, of course.

"Excuse me a second," I said. "I want to tell my pal where to meet me."

While she ankled over to the Buick, I went to the Ford and talked to Billy.

"Wait'll we drive off and then you follow. Keep a good distance back. Got it?"

"I got it. What I ain't got is th' suds ye been promisin' me."

"Later," I said.

"I'm dry." He coughed sadly into his cap.

"Suck on your hat for a while," I said.

I got into the Buick and the blonde gunned us away from the curb. I rolled down the window on my side and let the breezes blow on me.

"Nice car," I said. "Your husband's?"

She shook her head and that long coil of hair wiggled off her shoulder.

"It's a friend's car," she said. "Lovely color, don't you think, Lew?"

She worked my name into the conversation as easily as if we'd been buddies for years.

I returned the compliment. "It's sensational. And so are you, Agnes."

She wrinkled her nose at me. "Please, not that. My friends — my *intimate* friends — call me Sweetie."

"Am I an intimate friend?"

"Of course."

"Thank you, Sweetie."

She gave me another golden smile and turned onto Sixth Street. "Where shall we have that drink? My place all right? I fix a devilish Angel's Caress."

I nodded.

I sneaked a glance out the rear window, hoping to see Billy's headlights a respectable distance behind us. His distance was entirely too respectable; he was nowhere in sight.

She turned the lavender Buick off Sixth onto Atlantic and headed toward the beach.

"Your place near by?" I asked.

"Another block or so."

"Will we be . . .?" I hesitated deliberately. "Will anybody . . .?"

"My husband?" She laughed cheerfully. "That's just a little story I tell sometimes to keep the wolves from getting too frisky. I'm not married, of course."

She parked in front of a surrealistic-looking apartment house built in the form of an X and I couldn't help thinking it was a warning for me to be on the lookout for a double-cross. I was certain I was being led into a trap; everything pointed to it. She was being charming, she was throwing sex around like confetti and yet I knew darn well she was involved in all three killings up to her apricot-colored eyebrows. I wondered who she'd have lying in wait for me when we got upstairs. Kreena? Riki Tagsisi? Macapagal? Horondo?

As we walked under the long canvas canopy to the entrance, I gave a last glance over my shoulder for Billy. He was nowhere in view and I didn't like it a bit. I wished I'd had sense enough to bring along a gun.

We rode up to the fourth floor in a self-operated elevator and I had a tough time keeping a grinning, tomcat-on-the-town expression on my face. It was a small, compact elevator, its smooth walls pressed in on me closely and Sweetie's heavy perfume enveloped me like a radioactive cloud.

When we arrived at the door to her apartment, I was so much improved, however, that I decided to ask the question which had been bothering me.

"I wonder if you could do me a favor." I made it sound unimportant.

"Certainly." With a flourish she pushed the door open. "Enter, handsome."

"You lie like a mink rug," I said, "but thank you anyway. I was wondering if you could tell me where Riki Tagsisi went after you two left the Flowering Plum."

"Make yourself comfy." She gestured at a plush white velvet chesterfield and she strolled over to a built-in bar.

"I think Riki went downtown," she added. "In fact I'm sure of it. He has another job, you know. Works nights."

"No, I didn't," I said. "And I can't help wondering what your connection is with men like Riki and Felix." I paused. "And Oliver."

"Strictly business." She poured rum into two tall glasses and mixed in some liqueurs.

"They hardly seem your type," I said, hoping I wasn't sounding too persistent.

"Let's not talk shop." She sat down beside me on the white

velvet chesterfield and handed me a long, tall cool one.
"There you are, an Angel's Caress. Tell me how you like it."

I took a sip and decided it was mostly high-octane rum,
strong enough to walk on.

"Delicious," I said.

"Thank you." She smiled her golden smile. "I also serve this
kind of caress."

Leaning close, she rubbed her cheek softly against mine
and then brushed her lips across my chin.

And suddenly I didn't care if she had mickeyed up my
drink. I drained it to the bottom, set the glass down on the
coffee table and wrapped my arms around her.

I kissed her and she sighed and closed her eyes, making
it easier to sneak a glance around the room. I adjusted our
position on the divan slightly, enabling me to keep the front
door and the bedroom and dinette doors under surveillance.
It wasn't a very chivalrous thing to do, of course, but I
had to keep alert in case one of her business associates
should suddenly appear. I felt uncomfortable about the front
door being closed, but she was doing a lot of interesting
things to keep my attention more localized.

"Ummmmmmmm," she said. "What a wonderful way to
spend a night off."

"You work every night?" I asked.

She nuzzled my ear. "Some weeks I do."

"What sort of work do you do?"

"Let's not talk shop." She sighed. "Pucker up."

I found it very difficult to think clearly. Part of my brain
wanted to ask her a batch of questions and the other part —
the most demanding part — insisted that I make at least a
tentative move toward slipping her black shirt off.

She made the decision for me.

"How about another Caress?" she asked. "I mean in a
glass?"

As she got up, she left her shirt in my lap.

I couldn't figure out how she'd done it. We'd been doing a lot of squirming, but not that much.

She pranced barefooted over to the bar and began mixing two more drinks. All she had on were the black Capri pants and a lavender bra and her figure was elegant. She was slim-waisted and in this new perspective I saw that her frontal shelf was in perfect proportion with the rest of her.

"You go in for lavender," I said. "Your favorite color, I suppose?"

"Not especially," she said.

"I knew a man once that liked lavender." I made it sound merely conversational. "Maybe you've heard of him — a guy named Kreena?"

"No," she said.

Her face was too far away for me to see her expression, but her answer was enough. The single word *no* had been a little too carefully composed.

"He sometimes uses the first name of Carlos," I added.

She returned, handed me a glass and made a face. "Carlos, Schmarlos — who cares? Let's talk about something more interesting, like sin after dark or sin before breakfast or perhaps sin in the afternoon."

"Why not every hour on the hour?" I asked.

"You're cute." She rubbed her nose against my cheek. "But aren't you bragging, just a little? I mean — oh, I nearly forgot."

She sat up straighter on the divan and pointed her mother-of-pearl painted fingernail at me. "I mean, it was you who forgot."

"Forgot what?"

"The key. You forgot to give me Felix's key."

She held out her hand, palm up.

"You're misquoting me," I said. "I didn't say I'd give it to you. I said I'd be glad to talk about it."

"Don't be technical." She began twirling the loop of blond

hair and the rhythmical motion of her arm set up a corres-
ponding rhythm within the lavender bra which was fabulous,
to say the least. "Of course, you'll give it to me."

"Of course," I said.

What else could I say? Besides, I knew I could probably
sneak another key from Lowney if I had to.

So I drew it from my pocket.

She held her drink in one hand and she was twirling the
loop with the other, leaving me with a bit of a problem.

"Where shall I put it?" I asked.

"Where do you suppose?"

She filled her lungs with air and thrust her bra toward me.
"Oooooh." She shivered. "It's cold."

"Sorry," I said. "Want me to warm it up?"

I reached back toward her bra, but she slid away from
me confirming what I'd suspected all along. She hadn't forgotten the key, not for an instant. It had been uppermost in
her mind during the ride in the Buick and during her flatter-
ing capers in and out of the black shirt.

She turned away from me, ostensibly to place her glass
down, but I could tell by the way she hunched forward
momentarily that she had slipped the key from her bra.

I didn't like her secretiveness. I decided to take the key
away from her and use it to pry out the secret. If the key
were as important as I thought, she might be willing to
talk about it in exchange for having it returned.

I grabbed her hand, the one that was tightly closed around
the key.

She let out a little cry. "Please! You're hurting me!"

As I started to bend her wrist, the door chimes rang.

"Please, Lew!" Her golden brown eyes looked at me im-
ploringly. "Let me answer it. It's important!"

She began to weep.

I've always been a fool about feminine tears.

I released her.

She slipped swiftly into the black shirt, tucked it into the black Capri pants and sped to the door. It opened inward, concealing her caller from my view, but I could tell by the low voice that it was a man.

They spoke only a few words and then Sweetie hurried to a walk-in closet. In a moment she reappeared carrying a brown paper sack.

I rose from the white chesterfield and followed her silently, approaching in such a way that the door kept them from seeing me.

Through the crack between the door and the jamb I got an excellent look at the man to whom she had handed the paper sack.

He was about six foot three, he had a face the shape of a ukele and I knew his name as well as my own.

Macapagal.

He turned and walked along the hall, holding the sack as if it were the most important thing in his life.

Sweetie closed the door and then gasped as she discovered me standing about two feet away.

I shoved her aside, opened the door and strode down the hall after Macapagal.

I was so full of curiosity about that sack that I could taste it.

CHAPTER XIV

MACAPAGAL beat me to the elevator by about ten yards and vanished behind its closing doors. Remembering my queasy previous trip in that crackerbox, I didn't mind a bit. I found the stairway and bounced down the steps two, three, and four at a time.

When I reached the main floor, he was near the lobby's glass front doors.

I yelled at him. "Hey, Mac!"

It was informal, but it worked.

He stopped and turned around.

When he saw me, his dark face grew darker with distress and he sprinted the rest of the way to the glass doors.

I got there at the same time. I grabbed his arm and dragged him to a halt.

He didn't appreciate me at all. He looked down at me with exquisite contempt.

"Sir," he boomed in deep Oxford tones, "get your grubby hands off!"

I shook my head. "Let me see what's in the bag."

He tried to squirm away. "Release me, or I'll shout for help!"

I didn't reply. I squeezed his elbow with my fingers, digging them in deep and hard, using all my strength, which is considerable.

His expression of exquisite contempt was replaced by an expression of exquisite pain.

He dropped the brown paper sack neatly at my feet.

I picked it up and looked inside.

It contained half a dozen packages of firecrackers.

And I could feel an expression of exquisite confusion on my face.

"I hope you're satisfied," Macapagal said. "They're for my nephew's birthday. We shoot them off every year."

I didn't buy that at all.

"Why'd you try to run?" I demanded. "And why was your errand so important that you wind up at midnight at a blonde's apartment? Firecrackers? Who do you think you're kidding? What was the big deal you and Sweetie were mumbling about up there?"

"Sir, your inquires bore me."

He reached for the bag. I had no intention of giving it

to him, but unfortunately I saw a side door open in the
lobby and a man came in.

Correction, a human blimp came in.

It was my friend Mr. Horondo, the business opportunities
broker. He stepped into the elevator.

He couldn't have picked a more inconvenient time to
show up.

I didn't say another word to Macapagal. I stuffed half the
firecrackers in my pocket, tossed him what was left in the
bag and sprinted back to the stairway.

The first thing I learned was that it's a lot harder to
run upstairs than down. Horondo had gotten off at Sweetie's
floor.

I hid myself behind a plastic decorator screen and watched
him walk directly toward Sweetie's door.

But he didn't stop.

He continued almost to the end of the hall, got out a
key and opened a door to another apartment.

But he didn't go in.

For a moment he stood there thoughtfully pressing a
pudgy finger into the suet layers of his cheek.

Then he came back down the hall, wiggling with every
step.

And this time my old huncheroo was right. He stopped in
front of Sweetie's door and rang the chimes.

The door opened, but he didn't go in. Nor did Sweetie
come out. Her hand gracefully deposited something on his
palm, they spoke a few low words together and then the
door closed and Horondo trudged back down the hall.

I was getting darned tired of being left out of all of
Sweetie's fascinating conversations.   ‘

And I had a skulking suspicion that the object she'd
placed on Horondo's palm was an oriental key.

I waited until he went into the other apartment and then
I returned to her door and punched the chimes' button.

She didn't answer. I tested the doorknob; it was locked.

I jabbed the button again. Then I hit it three times in succession. That didn't work either. I knew she was in there and it was insultingly obvious that she had guessed I was paying a return call.

I strolled along the hall to the door where Horondo had entered and debated paying him a call. I decided it would be premature. First I needed information from Sweetie; after that I could get down to brass facts with Horondo.

Retracing my steps along the hall, I stopped in front of a door located midway between Sweetie's door and Horondo's. It was a white-enameled door minus an apartment number and its very plainness intrigued me. It was locked, of course. I dropped to my knees and studied the lock closely.

It was a dark, off-shade brass color and there was no manufacturer's brand visible. Tiny, fresh scratches in the white-enameled panel indicated that the lock could've been installed quite recently.

I felt a flush of triumph. This was the lock that Felix's and King Harold's keys fitted. Sweetie had staged a flabbergasting performance to get one of those keys and had promptly turned it over to Horondo. Moreover, the door was located significantly between Sweetie's apartment and Horondo's.

I had a colossal yen to see what was behind that door.

I went downstairs to a phone booth in the lobby and called Sergeant Phister at the cop shop. After some convincing, Phister agreed to "borrow" the other oriental key from King Harold's file. I gave him the address of the apartment house and told him I'd be out front waiting. I suggested that he send it in a plain black patrol car.

It was a far longer wait than I expected. I sat on a bus bench out front of the building for a while, observing the few people that went in and out. Since I'd already spotted Macapagal and Horondo on the premises, it seemed logical that Kreena and Riki Tagsisi might show up too, but I had no such luck. I examined the yellow and red firecrackers I'd taken from Macapagal, breaking open a few and pouring the silver powder they contained into my palm. I shredded the paper wadding between my fingers, but I couldn't discover anything unusual. I decided to let Lowney run a lab test on them.

For a while I counted cars, hoping I might spot Billy driving by, but that was too much to ask for. I went back inside and dialed my office on the chance he might be there, but that didn't pay off either.

Finally, at one forty-five in the morning, a police car pulled up and a plainclothes John got out.

"You Lew Pool?" he asked.

"Yeah. You got the key?"

He scowled as he handed it to me. "Phister had me make a duplicate. What kind of crazy key is it, anyway? It didn't match our stock no how."

"Sorry," I said. "I hope it works."

"Want me to come along and help jiggle it?"

"Good idea," I said. "Thanks."

We went up to the fourth floor and of course the damn key didn't work.

"Holy cows!" exploded the John. "How do you —"

I cautioned him to be quiet.

"That ain't the lock for this key," he whispered angrily.

I didn't know what to say. I was stumped.

The John frowned and cursed and then got out a ring of pass keys large enough to choke a mastodon. He worked with the finesse of an accomplished crook, silently trying key after key. When the tumblers clicked I could have kissed him, Phister, Lowney and the rest of the force.

"You want me to come in with you?" he whispered.

I shook my head. "I can handle the rest of it."

I pushed open the door, stepped inside and closed it behind me.

I stood in the darkness for a full minute without moving, listening. I gritted my teeth and kept the claustro heebie jeebies from getting a firm grip on me. When I was certain I was alone, I felt quietly along the wall for a light switch. For a change my luck was good. The switch I found had a mercury unit and there was no sound as it filled the room with light.

I blinked.

And I was certain I was closer to Kreena than I had been all day.

I was surrounded by heliotrope and lavender. The walls were lavender, the shag rug was lavender, the ceiling was lavender and the two overstuffed chairs were lavender, too.

The bed was king-sized, with a shiny satin lavender spread. Its lavender blankets were turned back, revealing lavender sheets and lavender pillows.

It was all pretty sickening.

CHAPTER XV

I STOOD there for perhaps another minute studying the geography of the place, smelling the too-sweet fragrance of a triangle of lavender incense burning in a metal cup near the bed.

I noted that there were two doors, one leading to Sweetie's apartment, the other to Horondo's.

Very convenient.

Extinguishing the light, I moved quietly across the room and eased open Sweetie's door.

I passed through a pink-tiled bathroom, opened another door and looked into a conventional bedroom. Sweetie was nowhere in sight.

I waited, but heard no movement anywhere in the apartment. Leaving the bedroom, I walked along a hall into the living room. A lamp was burning near the white velvet chesterfield, but there was still no sign of Sweetie. I wondered if she had gone to Horondo's apartment.

I crossed the living room and went into the walk-in closet where Sweetie had obtained the bag of firecrackers which she had given Macapagal. On a shelf above a rack of coats and dresses were piled numerous packages of firecrackers. I tore open a package and broke half a dozen firecrackers in two. They contained nothing more significant than silver powder.

Moving deeper into the closet, I accidentally kicked over a shoebox, knocking off its cover and spilling its heavy brass contents onto the floor.

As soon as I picked up the pieces of brass I knew I'd found something important.

They were the sections of a dissembled lock, made of dark oriental-looking metal. I drew out the key that the John had given me, the duplicate of King Harold's and inserted it in the keyhole.

It fitted perfectly and operated the mechanism.

There was absolutely no doubt in my mind that the lock had been installed in the door to the lavender room and only recently removed.

As I started to turn around and stand up, I caught a glimpse of someone standing behind me. It was Sweetie and she swung something at me with vicious accuracy.

I've mentioned before that she was a large girl. She swung that object with tremendous force. It caught me on the top of my head just as I started to straighten up, adding unnecessary impact to the blow.

I went down as if I'd been hit by a train.

I didn't pass out but I would have been better off if I had.

I was sure my scalp and half my brains had been scattered liberally around the closet. The pain was so great it paralyzed me. Unable to move my arms or legs, I lay flat on my back and felt a vast amount of warm and sticky fluid ooze across my temple. It scared the hell out of me because I knew I didn't have that much blood to spare. Eventually a trickle reached my mouth and I was forced to taste it.

It was rum. That damn woman had belted me with that big bottle of rum.

I don't know how long I lay there in the darkness. Finally Stage I passed and I entered Stage II in which I was able to move my hands and feet and brush some of the broken glass off my shoulders. I managed to ease myself into a sitting position, but even that slow careful movement made my head shake with a fantastic agony. I dragged myself to the door and gripped the knob.

It was locked. Despite the pain in my head, I thrust my shoulders against the door.

I was too weak and the door was too strong and that was the beginning of Stage III.

It was terror.

It was desolation, it was purgatory, it was all the misery I had ever known in my lifetime.

I couldn't get out.

I screamed as I felt the lice creeping on me and I felt the darkness of the hole all around me and I smelled the stench of myself fourteen months in that hole and I knew I must be crazy . . . but I couldn't convince myself that I wasn't back there because my brain was being squeezed and squeezed and squeezed by that closed door, that closed door, that closed . . .

I passed out.

When I came out of it an unknown interval of time later, the terror was no less, but I had regained a small amount of intelligence, enough to know where I was. I hurled myself at the door, but I was too nauseous and the panel felt like it was made of boiler plate.

I slipped exhausted to the floor and there was only one thought in my mind, only one thought that kept me semi-intact. Kreena was doing this to me. Kreena had reduced me to this ridiculous watery weakness. I concentrated on him. I concentrated all my hatred on him. I thought about what I would do to him, I thought about all the desperate things I would do to him. I though about how I would enjoy killing him. It helped; I wished it could have helped more, but it was better than nothing.

More time passed and then the door opened quickly and someone came stumbling in.

Before I could rise and seize it, the door was slammed shut and locked.

A man tripped on my legs in the darkness and fell on top of me.

He rolled off, yelling and complaining, and as soon as I heard that brogue I felt a thousand times better.

"Shades o' Kilarney!" he cried. "A dead body! 'Tis a dead —"

"Relax!" I said. "I'm only seven-eighths a corpse hardly enough to bother with. Hurry up and open the door!"

"Lew!" Billy exclaimed. "Sure an' 'tis it really you?"

He clapped his arm around me and it felt damn good.

"Open the door!" I said.

"Sure, Lew, sure!" He clucked his tongue sympathetically. "Ye poor fella. Ye must be nearly out o' yer mind!"

He didn't know how right he was.

He yanked on the knob, he battered his shoulder against the panel for five minutes but he couldn't get the door to budge.

" 'Tis solid!" he raged. " 'Tis solid as the U. S. S. Sullivan!"

He tried again, panting and puffing, and making no headway whatsoever.

" 'Tis me bum leg!" he complained. "Keeps me from gettin' leverage!"

I could feel the heebie jeebies closing in on me again. I needed something to concentrate on.

"Talk to me, Billy," I said. "Where in the blazes did you disappear to? And how did you let yourself get trapped in here?"

"Ye should talk, Lew" he said. "As fer what happened, I hung back like ye said and th' first thing I knew that fruity-colored Buick was plumb out o' sight. So I drove 'round an' 'round lookin' fer ye. Finally I spots th' Buick parked out front so I come in th' lobby here and starts lookin' around and then that fella with th' big backside caught me. Ye know th' one, Lew. He looks like th' hind end o' a Greyhound bus."

"Horondo?" I said.

"Yeah. He waves a gun under me nose, brings me up here an' locks me in. I'm sure sorry I let ye down, Lew."

"It's okay," I said. "Keep talking."

"What'll I talk about?"

"Anything."

"Well . . ." He sniffed. "What's that funny smell?"

"Rum," I said.

"No, not that," Billy said. "That powdery smell. Fire-crackers?"

"Yeah. I broke open a few."

"I did too," Billy said. "While I was drivin' around, I tried shootin' some. Half went off, half didn't and I found out them yella ones are no damn good an' only the red ones worked. There's something fishy about them yella ones, Lew."

"How do you mean?"

"They got th' same kind o' silver powder but it only looks th' same. I tasted that powder an' it was different. It tasted fishy."

I sat on the floor for another minute, thinking about the

firecrackers and then I tried getting to my feet. I was weak and sick and every movement made me feel sicker and weaker. But I knew that if we didn't make another try at that door, neither of us would leave the closet alive.

I lost my balance and fell against Billy.

"What are ye' tryin' to do?"

"Let's give that door another try," I grunted. "Let's hit it together."

I figured I had strength for maybe three attempts. We backed up as far as we could and then ran for all we were worth. Correction: Billy ran, while I sort of stumbled.

We hit it and bounced off.

We did it five or six times and I swore each time that I was too sick and exhausted to make another try.

And then a split appeared in the panel and through it I saw a glimmer of light from the living room.

Give a guy in my condition a glimmer from the great outside and you give him a tonic, you give him vitamins and minerals, you revitalize his tired blood.

I backed up until my spine touched the wall. I charged. I hit that glimmer of light with every ounce of my hundred and eighty-five pounds.

I tore a hell of a hole in the door.

I hit it again and this time I crashed through, scattering wood like cornflakes.

When I picked myself up from the rug, the first thing I saw was Sweetie sitting in a chair aiming a big Army-style .45 at me.

After what I'd been through, that pistol was an insignificant nothing. I filled my lungs with fresh air and freedom and launched myself at her.

Sweetie's mouth became a perfect, red-tinted O.

She fired once and then I knocked the pistol from her hand, upset her chair and we landed together in a jungle of wrists and ankles.

I untangled myself from her and stood up.

"Terrific, Lew!" Billy exclaimed. " 'Twas th' bravest thing ever I seen th' way ye faced th' gun!"

"I was lucky," I said.

"Next time don't be so brave," he added. "Th' damn bullet missed me nose by no more'n a whisper!"

"Sorry." I glanced around the living room. "I thought you said Horondo was out here."

"I heard him say he was leavin'. He was goin' after that Ricky-ticky fella."

"Riki Tagsisi?"

"Yeah."

"Okay," I said, "we'll be ready for 'em. Pick up the gun and get over to the front door. Soon as you hear 'em in the hall give me the word."

He retrieved the pistol from under a white leather hassock and stationed himself at the door.

"We've some talking to do," I said.

Sweetie was now sitting on the rug, rubbing her shoulder.

"I've nothing to say to you," she said. "You —"

I distracted her by dragging her across the floor and depositing her, stomach down, on the white velvet chesterfield.

"What's in the firecrackers?" I demanded.

"Go fry your hat," she told me sweetly.

"I'll beat it out of you," I warned.

"You wouldn't dare."

I slapped her on the rump and she yelped with pain.

"What's in the firecrackers?" I said.

"I don't know!"

I knew she didn't have a thing on under those Capri pants. And that black cloth, stretched as tight as her skin, didn't give her a dab of protection. I slapped her again, harder, my palm giving off a very satisfactory sound.

"Damn you, damn you, damn you!" she said.

I hit her twice more and for the first time her yells sounded genuine.

"You know all about the firecrackers!" I said. "You know about everything else, too!"

I kept smacking the same rounded area again and again and I could tell by the way she rolled about, trying to dodge, that it was getting sore.

I kept asking the same question.

She wept, she bounced around on the chesterfield like a lady wrestler, she kicked at me, she tried to bite me and through it all I kept pounding away on that same spot.

When her resistance finally broke, she spouted words in a torrent that I couldn't understand.

"It's *Bebaselo!*" she shrieked. "*Bebaselo! Bebaselo!*"

"What?" I smacked her again. "What did you say?"

"Stop, stop, stop!" she wept. "It's a drug! *Bebaselo!* It's a powder in the firecrackers!"

Well, that was more like it.

I raised my hand as if to strike her again and she spouted more words.

It's amazing what a little psychology can do when it's applied right.

CHAPTER XVI

"It's made out of powdered fish scales!" she shrieked.

Again I raised my hand. "And what else?"

"I don't know what else! It's made in the Philippines! It's shipped here by boat, a few packages at a time!"

"What's it used for?"

"I don't know!"

I moved my hand toward her.

"Don't!" she yelled. "Don't hit me again! It's put in whiskey or gin or rum or any liquor!"

"Tell me more," I said.

She calmed down a little, drying her eyes on her sleeve. Her face was a mess, the mascara streaks making her look like she'd been belted with a coal shovel.

"Only a tiny amount is mixed with the liquor," she said. "It's tasteless."

"What's the effect?"

"It's makes people drink more."

"What else does it do?"

She shrugged. "Isn't that enough? They can have a dozen cocktails, a dozen whiskies and never feel 'em. They just get thirstier and keep ordering more without ever getting drunk. They feel swell. It triples the business at any bar."

I didn't need to have it explained any further. No wonder there had been such a crowd in Macapagal's cocktail lounge. No wonder he'd been willing to come around at midnight for a new supply.

"How much of it's being distributed?"

She shrugged again. "I don't know. Lots. He's been sending plenty to places in San Diego, San Francisco and Seattle. He'll be spreading East pretty soon, to Chicago and New York."

"Who do you mean by *he*?"

"Can't you guess?"

It wasn't too difficult. Macapagal couldn't be the distributor because he'd had to come to Sweetie to pick up a supply for his place. Besides, I'd seen a pile of firecrackers in Horondo's office so the answer was obvious.

"Horondo?" I said.

She nodded.

"Does he pick the stuff up from the boat?"

"Sometimes. Sometimes he sends one of the boys."

I remembered the newspaper clipping I'd seen among Felix's effects at the jail. It told of the arrival of the S.S. Caledonia from the Philippines.

"Did Felix pick up the last load?"

"I suppose so."

"There's something about this you haven't told me," I said. "What makes the drug so illegal? Is it dangerous?"

"Of course." She eased herself up to a sitting position, wincing as the tender area contacted the white velvet cushion.

"What does it do?"

"Drink it for a year or so and it'll rot out your liver."

It was a very pleasant little after-effect, exactly the kind of vicious thing a man like Kreena would be involved in.

"You're doing fine," I said, "but you haven't told me what Kreena's connection is. Does he ship the stuff to Horondo — or vice versa?"

"Kreena?" She gave me a dumb-blonde look.

"Come on," I said. "He's in this and you know it."

I raised my hand and she slid away from me, cowering and moaning as her bottom rubbed across the cushions.

"Kreena's a killer," I said. "He killed Felix, didn't he?"

"I don't know anything about that," she said. "I told you everything I know."

It was a very poor lie.

She jumped off the divan and made a dash toward the bedroom. I caught her before she'd gone six steps and dragged her back to the chesterfield.

I slapped her once. That was all it took. One good one in that tenderized region.

"Riki did it!" she screamed. "Riki killed Felix!"

"How?" I demanded.

"He works nights in the jail. He's a cook. He had a gun hidden in the pots and pans!"

It was so logical it astounded me and I wondered why I hadn't had sense enough to spot the setup myself.

"Why'd he do it?" I said. "What was the motive?"

She didn't reply.

Her golden brown eyes had suddenly grown large and round with fright.

She wasn't looking at me. She was looking at someone behind me.

"Why bother her?" said a soft, furry masculine voice. "Why not ask me?"

I didn't like his tone. I didn't like it at all and I turned around slowly, not taking any chances.

A small, thin Filipino stood there holding not one but two pistols. He had a narrow face that was all bone and his eyes were so intensely black they looked like hot tar. He wore black trousers and a sport shirt made of shiny lavender satin.

I recognized him from his picture. Riki Tagsisi, of course.

Behind him stood Billy, holding his cap in his hands, looking downcast and ashamed of himself.

Behind Billy stood Horondo, armed with a .38 revolver.

"I let ye down, Lew," Billy said forlornly. "I was guardin' th' door like ye said but they come in a different way —"

"It's not your fault," I said. "It's mine."

I had definitely goofed. I'd been so busy with Sweetie I'd forgotten about the entrance through the lavender room.

Riki Tagsisi came a step closer and I saw that the gun in his left hand was the Army pistol Billy had been holding. He was the most intense little man I'd ever seen. His face was stiff with tension and the muscles on his thin arms stood out in stringy ridges and narrow humps.

He moved like he was walking on exposed nerve ends.

He stopped in front of Sweetie.

"You shouldn't have said that," he told her quietly. "What happened at the jail is my business."

Behind the mascara streaks, her face was dead white. "I'm sorry, Riki —"

"You will *never* do that again," he said.

"Of course not, Riki."

Horondo came closer. "Leave her alone, Riki. Attend to the others."

Riki Tagsisi ignored him. He swung his right hand savagely and the pistol sight cut a brilliant red slash in her cheek.

"Riki!" Horondo said, "I'm warning you . . ."

Riki struck her again.

And Horondo shot him twice in the back.

The tension left Riki Tagsisi quickly and effortlessly.

He fell forward onto the white rug and lay without moving, one brown hand touching Sweetie's bare foot.

She recoiled, lifting her legs onto the chesterfield.

"Thank god!" Her voice was perhaps two notes below hysteria. "Thank god, Carlos!"

Horondo aimed the revolver at me.

"All right, sergeant," he said. "All right."

I stood there like an imbecile, wondering what chance I had to get one of the guns that Riki Tagsisi had fallen upon.

Horondo fired and metal sailed close to me and exploded a porcelain figure on the mantel.

And then Billy nonchantly slipped off his artifical leg and calmly used it like a club, knocking the pistol from Horondo's hand.

Horondo couldn't believe it and neither could I.

Horondo stooped to pick up the pistol and Billy, standing there like a one-legged crane, whacked him over the head with the shoe at the end of the detached limb.

I kicked Horondo's pistol across the floor.

"Pick 'em up!" I shouted to Billy. "Pick up all three!"

Billy hopped over and seized Horondo's pistol and then hopped to Riki Tagsisi and seized the other two guns.

For a moment I didn't move. I looked at Horondo's ugly round face and his swollen round body and I knew who he was.

I knew that Sweetie had called him Carlos. And that was

the name of the fifth man in the picture Felix's sister had shown me.

And he had called me sergeant.

I looked at him and saw how he had chosen to hide himself under layers of fat and the sight of him made me sick.

Fat Stuff could tell by my face what I was going to do and he broke for the door.

I grabbed him by the collar of his gray silk shantung coat and turned him around.

I hit him in that great belly and he squealed at me. I hit him again and it was like driving my fist into something soft and rotten that had been lying around a butcher shop too long.

I sat in one of the white chairs for a few minutes, re-organizing my thoughts and wiping my knuckles with a handkerchief.

I grinned at Billy. "You were terrific. When you hit him with your leg I thought his eyeballs would pop out."

Billy grinned back sheepishly. " 'Twas th' least I could do fer ye, Lew. Ye think maybe I earned meself a six-pack?"

"Possibly," I, said. "Possibly a whole case."

I left the chair and walked over to the white velvet chester-field.

Sweetie hadn't moved. She wore a dazed expression. She also wore a streak of blood on her nose that made her look ridiculous and stupid.

"You going to tell me about it?" I said.

Her mouth turned downward sullenly. "Tell you what?"

"There's more to it than the drug," I said. "Lot's more."

"I've told you enough," she said.

"There's only one way out for you," I said. "You're going to have to tell everything. You're going to have to charm that jury like no jury was ever charmed before."

That got to her.

She sat up straight, preening herself. She straightened the black shirt and tucked the loop of blond hair into the lavender bra. She didn't know it, but with that blood on her face, plus the streaked mascara, she looked as unpreened as a pullet with its head in a fan.

"I'll charm 'em." She winked at me. "I'll charm the hell out of 'em."

"Start at the beginning," I said. "I want to know all about your business association with the Manilas. I want to know about this job of yours and I want to know about the keys and the lavender room."

"Certainly," she said. "Certainly."

"But before you get into that," I said. "I want to know something else. Did Ti-lo have anything to do with the *Bebaselo?*"

"Of course not. Only a few of us knew about it."

She didn't know what a relief her words were.

"Okay," I said, "now get on with the rest of it."

She took a cigarette from the white box on the table. I let her light it by herself.

"It started about four months ago," she said. "I was a little low on money because business had slipped. It was then that these five little gentlemen happened to contact me. We negotiated for almost a week before we agreed on terms which were mutually satisfactory."

"What kind of terms?" I said.

"Very excellent terms." She tapped the ash from her cigarette into a tray. "I was to have the house on El Portal, of course. And they were each to pay me ninety-five dollars a week."

"A week?" I said. "Each guy?"

"Of course. I tried to make it one hundred even but they couldn't afford it." She giggled. "As it was, they had to get extra jobs to keep up the payments."

"Pretty stiff payments," I said. "What were they for?"

She giggled again. "Silly. For me, of course! They each spent one night a week with me." She smoothed her hair with a proud, feminine gesture. "They each had a key to the house. Tuesday was Felix's night. Wednesday was Oliver's, Thursday was King Harold's, Friday was Riki Tagsisi's, and Carlos Horondo had Saturday and Sunday nights. Monday was my night off."

She smiled brightly. "Mr. Horondo paid double, of course. He liked me the most."

"Use his right name," I said. "Kreena."

She shrugged. "Small difference."

"So what happened?" I said. "What caused this beautiful arrangement to break down?"

"It was inevitable, I suppose." She sighed dramatically. "Carlos, I mean Kreena, was very jealous of the others and after a while he didn't like the arrangement at all. And then he began making so much money from the *Bebaselo* that he could afford to spend every night with me. He tried to buy out the others, but they wouldn't sell."

She smiled again. "They liked me," she added. "They liked me so very, very much, but I did get bored with them after a while, so I didn't mind when Carlos, I mean Kreena, made his arrangement with Riki. He said Riki could continue to have Friday nights if he would help get rid of the others. Riki thought a great deal of Kreena, so he agreed."

We were silent for a minute while I analyzed what she had said. I thought back over the events of the long day and night and there were still some crazy elements that hadn't been fitted into the pattern.

"Was it Riki that tried to kill me by bombing my car at the Flowering Plum?"

"Yes," she said.

"Why?"

"Because Carlos, I mean Kreena, told him to. Kreena was afraid you'd recognize him."

I shook my head. "Not a chance. I wouldn't have recognized that slob in a hundred years."

She started to rise from the chesterfield.

"Stay where you are," I said. "We're not finished."

Her red lips pouted. "I need a drink."

"Forget it," I said. "So Riki killed them all, correct? Including King Harold who was still hanging around the house on El Portal trying to learn where you and the oriental lock had vanished to?"

"Yes," she said. "Now may I have that drink? I need it."

"In a minute. What was the deal with the lavender room?"

"That was to be just for Kreena and Riki." She lit a fresh cigarette and her mother-of-pearl tipped fingers were as steady as steel. "We changed the lock again tonight, in case the police should come with one of the boys' keys."

"One more question," I said. "Tell me, Sweetie, do you really think you were worth five hundred and seventy dollars a week?"

CHAPTER XVII

WHEN I phoned Inspector Lowney, he took it very well until I got to the part about how Riki Tagsisi was on the cop shop payroll.

For a minute the line snapped, crackled and popped. But then Inspector Lowney apologized to me.

I was almost overcome.

"Please stick around," he said. "We're coming right over."

It took him and a roomful of Johns two hours to sift the thing down. When they finished, their conclusions were the same as mine.

"How soon will you release Ti-lo?" I demanded.

"Immediately." Lowney looked at his wrist watch. "In half an hour.

I had a test to make.

Sergeant Winebrenner was back on duty and I gave him exactly twelve cigars, six for himself and six for Sergeant Phister.

"Break one more rule for me," I said. "I want to be in the women's section when they let her out."

He shook his head. "I don't know about that, Lew."

But he set it up, of course.

I followed a matron to the cell at the end of the barred corridor.

She was sitting on a cot, looking down at her hands clenched in her lap.

"Hi," I said.

She looked up, but she didn't say anything.

"Don't just sit there like a dummy," I said. "Come on out."

She watched the matron unlock the door but she still didn't accept it.

"Honest?" she asked.

I nodded. "Absolutely."

Her Irish blue eyes lit up like the morning sky and she came out in a rush and grasped my hands.

"Lew, I'll never be able to thank you! I'll just never be able —"

"You don't have to," I said. "Now watch, I want to show you something."

Stepping into the cell, I motioned to the matron. "Madam, would you kindly lock the door?"

She looked at me like I had cobbies in my head, but she did it.

I flopped onto the cot and put my hands comfortably behind my head.

I felt fine.

No heebie jeebies. No nausea. No bars closing in on me.

Ti-lo shrieked with delight. "You did it! You found Kreena and you beat up on him!"

I nodded.

"So everything's fine, isn't it?"

"All except one item." I rose from the cot. "Macapagal's going to the hoosegow, so you're out of a job."

Before she could be disappointed, I added: "How would you like the job of getting other people out? How would you like a job in a bail bond office?"

She smiled so brightly I just naturally had to reach through and pull her close to the bars.

I planted a big one on those lush lips.